WAITING FOR A TRAIN

BY

ANTHONY DAY

Published by Columbine Pictures Press
Copyright © 2017 Anthony Day and Columbine Pictures Press

ISBN: 0995555648
ISBN-13: 978-0995555648

For Lisa Rodgers

PREFACE

The bride wore white, the sun shone brightly and the bridesmaids looked so cute in their little turquoise dresses.

It was such a wonderful day.
So wonderful.
I could die.

1

Everything was quiet. Nothing stirred, no breeze, no birds, no traffic, no sound but for the constant ticking of the seconds of a large, round clock that hung above her head. A constant ticking, a reminder that time was passing, slipping, ebbing away and there was nothing she could do about it.

It was a large clock, green-metal body, suspended on a metal arm high in the cream-coloured wooden roof over the concrete platform. Its Roman numerals were black against the bright, white face and the three black hands showed the time.

It was 11:58.

She was standing on the platform, looking at the two rows of tracks. In the distance in both directions the tracks seemed to run straight, converging into one as they dipped from sight, lost to the curve of the earth, running along the cutting with its high embankment, over which the trees and shrubs hung looking down the slope to the rails and gravel below.

An endless line that seemed to come from or go to nowhere as there were no buildings, no phone masts, no pylons, no other signs of humanity in either direction. Just hills on the horizons and a track that vanished into the distance.

She looked around her. The station was a large, red-brick Victorian building, with a double door in the centre which led to the ticket hall and exit. At the far end there was a waiting room and café with its door onto the platform and nearer to her were the male and female toilets. All the doors and window frames were dark green but halfway up the iron pillars that ran along the centre of the platform, the colour changed to a light cream, the same as the ceiling and ironwork of the platform's roof.

The fence that ran along to the ends of the platform past the station was also cream with a green enamel sign in which in white was written the name of the place - Halt End.

After a brief pause, she made her way over to a seat at the far corner.

She had long blonde hair, tied back into a ponytail, pulled hard back from her oval face. She had pale-blue eyes and full lips. She was very thin, fair-skinned and with little make-up, which gave her a tomboy appearance in her baggy pullover, skinny jeans and battered canvas shoes, which she wore without socks.

She looked along the platform back towards the waiting room for a moment but the door stayed firmly shut. No one was inside, no one was coming. She was alone.

She took from her jeans back pocket a creased letter which she began to open out and read.

As she did so, she began to cry, her fragile emotions starting to take over, the frustration and the sense of lonely isolation wearing her down. She crumpled the letter in her hands and dropped it to the floor, burying her head into her hands.

'Why all the tears?'

She looked and to her joy she saw them standing there before her. The one who had spoken, John Stanger, was a tall, rugged man with a mop of loose, curly, brown hair, brown eyes and a ridiculously broad smile. He was about ten years older than her and like the other two was dressed in old jeans, rough training shoes and a sweatshirt. Next to him was Paul Still, the tallest of the three, a little younger than John, thin with short, closely cropped, jet-black hair and dark-brown eyes and just behind them both stood Joe Webber, a slightly chubby man, the same height as herself and of a similar age with a freckly face, blue eyes and short, thinning, limp, ginger hair.

'You're here!' she exclaimed wildly, as surprised as she was delighted to see them.

'We wouldn't miss this for the world!' John replied and she noticed the slight twinkle in his eye.

She looked up to the clock.

The time was now 11:33.

Maybe, just maybe, there was a chance.

2

Joe was walking down the narrow street. The pavements either side, just wide enough for a single person to walk along, flanked the road, just wide enough for a single car to drive down. Encroaching on him, their long shadows growing as the fading sunlight slunk behind them, were the tall rows of town houses in small blocks of their historical period. Their front doors opened onto the street, which was a mismatch of medieval, Tudor and Georgian stretching from the centre of the city to the Tannery and the old church. Along a lane at the end he could just see behind the trees that edged its graveyard.

His pace was fast. Ahead of him he could see the tight sweeping bend before the church lane and the street lamp with its bright white light behind an old frosted glass was beginning to slowly come up to full brightness.

Joe slowed as he passed two black-and-white posts at

the edge of the kerb before he crossed a narrow road to a small dead-end street and walked past a bow-fronted corner shop, the trendy Banana Room hairdressers, passing three more of those posts that hemmed him in close to the shop, and then picked up his stride again.

Though the breeze was blowing away from him and all the shop's windows were shut, on the street side at least, he could still smell the rotten egg of the ammonia used in the tanning process and he thanked his luck he didn't have to work there.

Even though it wasn't a cold night, he was wearing a long, black coat which he had open, letting it flap partly behind him like a Gothic cloak as he walked.

As he reached the bend, to his left the housing gave way to a large car park, to which he crossed the road and, hopping over the low wall, cut across to the entrance where opposite him, was the Cardinal's Cap pub.

He was smoking a cigarette, which he finished as he reached the pub door. To his left, was the large window with the brewery name etched into the lower half of the glass and above, wired tight so that it wouldn't move, hung the sign with the fat-faced cardinal in his red cap looking down approvingly at him, finger raised. He dropped the cigarette and stubbed it out before entering through the nearer of the narrow, frosted-glass double doors.

He stood in the doorway for a moment as the door closed slowly behind him and looked around the room.

The Cap, as it was affectionately known by its regulars, was an unusual pub in a city dominated by pubs as it was a place with a strong Gothic vibe. As Joe entered, the horseshoe bar which looked out onto the room faced him. Behind the bar, Steve the landlord, a tall man with Celtic tattoos, a goatee beard and earrings, served with his two Brides of Dracula barmaids, one so pale with bright-red lipstick she looked like she had just been resurrected that morning.

The room itself was given over to two distinct areas,

an open standing area dividing the seating from the bar and running, between the three pillars to the small half-height partition wall that screened off the lower part of two black toilet doors, and the small four-inch high platform, the stage area which reached almost as far back into the room as the toilet block.

Against the walls that ran from the alley leading to the beer garden, the garages of the nearby houses and the main street were all the tables, the round ones near the street side having chairs, the long rectangular types in a row of three with benches either side, creating a false set of snugs as they weren't partitioned from each other.

Everything was dark oak coloured. In the centre of the long tables were old wine bottles down which red-and-white candles over time had melted to create a pattern over the glass and in which the opposite colour to the previous candle now flickered.

The atmosphere was heavy with smoke and, peculiar to the Cap itself, the ceiling was covered with sheet music, now much faded into a dark stain of sepia by the years of tobacco smoke, but including some of the great works of a diverse spectrum of composers and artists, from Mozart, Bach and Beethoven to Jethro Tull, Queen, Deep Purple, Siouxsie and the Banshees, Bauhaus, Killing Joke, The Selector and The Doors.

The pub was also full of Goths wearing long coats, the last surviving punks, and lovers of heavy metal. On the stage a heavy-rock girl and her three male band-mates were setting up for their gig.

Other regulars with their pints nodded their hellos on seeing Joe enter. There was an awful squeal of feedback from one of the band's amps and, as the sound died down, the rocker girl apologised and the crowd cheered, raising their glasses as if in honour.

There was other gothic and metal memorabilia around the room, like upturned crosses on the pillars and on the walls, a Madonna at prayer, horse bits, plaster skulls, and the odd black rose. Beside the silently flashing gaming machine next to the door, there was a notice-board on which was a jumble of flyers advertising forthcoming bands and the weekly quiz night with its rewards of a two-pint stein of either beer or larger to each member of the winning team and chocolate for the runners-up.

There was a hugely warm and friendly atmosphere there, unlike most other pubs in town and, although he himself was a bit of a closet Goth, those he had come to see were too Britpop at their most radical to be at home here.

He began to smile as he saw John and Paul talking at the far long table, next to the toilet divide, and quickly came over to them.

'... The point is,' John explained, 'she did have the keys and I mean, alright, keys are keys, but these keys do have a red cap on them.'

'Did she give them back in the end?'

As Joe arrived, he noticed that they already had their drinks.

'Hi there.'

'What kept you?' Paul asked.

'Had to run my younger sister to ballet.' Joe shrugged.

'Thought there had to be some reason for you not to be here,' John replied as Paul added, 'We thought that as soon as we arrived.'

'Eh?' Joe was confused.

'They still had beer!' Paul replied as Joe rolled his eyes.

'Sod you then,' he grinned. 'I'm going to get a pint. Ruth not here yet?'

'She rang me before setting off. She should be here in an hour or so,' John replied.

'Did she say how it went?' he asked hovering between leaving to get his pint and getting all the gossip.

'Apparently...' Paul began turning to John as if to check he'd got his facts right. 'What was it you said?'

'She said,' John continued, 'it went sweetly. Apparently the bride looked wonderful.'

Joe sighed.

'Don't they always? It's just like birthdays.'

'I don't see the similarity,' Paul challenged.

'The gifts look fine all wrapped up, but once you've used them a few times, it's to the bottom of the drawer, never to see the light of day again.'

'I thought you were getting a drink?' John reminded him.

'Yeah,' Joe glanced to the bar. 'Anyone want anything whilst I'm up?'

'No, we're fine,' Paul replied, holding his pint but leaving it resting on the table.

'See you in a mo.' And Joe headed to the bar.

'He's got a cynical attitude to marriage!' Paul sighed.

'Have a heart. He's only twenty-one!'

'I was engaged then!' Paul sighed again as he took a sip of his beer.

'It was all different then. I mean, we used to wear black, shiny suits and dance to ska. Nowadays they wear what we used to wear to work as their best.'

'What do you mean, used to?'

'Cheers.' John raised his glass taking a sip.

'I suppose he's cynical because he's not happily married like you,' John remarked as he placed his pint back down on the table.

'Well, when you've made love to the twelve-inch version of Wings of a Dove by Madness, why would anyone want anyone else?!'

'True?!!' John shrugged. 'I suppose. But then I always preferred One Step Beyond.'

'Well, there's your problem, mate. It's too short!' Paul grinned.

'Hey, watch it!'

Paul sipped his beer. 'So then?' Paul began. 'Did Julie give you back your keys at last?'

'Had too.'

'At least you never married her.'

Joe returned and sat on a stool between the other two at the head of the table.

'Came close though....' John admitted. 'I really felt as though I could have done. It's strange I've always felt as though I should get married some day, but you know...'

'I know. They all like raves rather than reggae these days!' Joe chipped in, in a light mocking way as Paul stood. Joe turned to him. 'Why didn't you ask me while I was up? There's a hell of a queue.'

'I don't want another pint just yet.'

'Eh?'

'I want to get rid of one.' Paul slipped out from behind the table and made his way over to the shabby black door.

'Weird, isn't it?' Joe sighed.

'What is?'

'It's weird how for every pint you drink, I'd swear you piss out two.' John grinned then sipped his pint. 'You say, Ruth will be here in an hour or so?'

'By eight.'

'So when are we heading up the club?'

'After she's had a drink and told us all about her cousin's wedding.'

'What!' Joe sighed regretfully. 'That'll mean we won't be in before eleven. We'll have to pay full price!'

3

The little old Mini slowed as it reached the end of the narrow country lane, either side of it the high verges, lined by a row of mature trees forming a tunnel of branches, making the early evening twilight seem all the darker.

Pulling up at the broken white lines across the junction, the engine idled. Caught in the beam of the little car's round headlamps, the crossroads stretched out in the three other directions.

Her long slender fingers flicked forward the little black button in the roof by her rear-view mirror and the interior light came on, illuminating the whole inside of the car. After unfastening her seatbelt, she reached across to the passenger side and pulled a large road atlas from the glove shelf on the other side of the single round speedometer and its four long black switches that made up the control panel sitting in the divide between the two seats.

'Bloody shortcuts!' She cursed herself as she opened the book out onto the passenger seat at the page she'd marked with her scribbled note to meet the boys at the Cap.

She cursed herself again. She knew she was going to be late.

She was lost and felt even worse, uncomfortable in her loose, pale-blue dress. She didn't like wearing dresses at the best of times, but this was just a little too short to reach over her knees and even though she was alone, she still felt the need to pull at the hem a little to see if she could stretch it.

On the rear bench seat, her white handbag and matching, wide-brimmed hat lay and, like the dress, were now destined to sit at the back of the wardrobe until the next 'special occasion' should arise.

She flicked through a couple of pages until she came to the area she was in and then after a quick glance up to the white signpost with its black lettering on each pointer, one for each of the roads, she found her place in the book and traced the road along to where she knew she should be.

She looked at her watch and growled, frustrated with herself, and cursed herself for deviating from her well-rehearsed plan. But then she always felt uncomfortable at weddings, especially turning up to them alone as she felt all those prying eyes watching her, and then having to spend the whole time justifying why it wasn't her big day or why she was there alone. She just wanted to be around friends or, at least, sane people. She slammed the book shut and wedged it again on the passenger-side glove shelf.

She turned off the interior light, clipped in place her seatbelt and in one move thrust the car into gear, let off the handbrake and put her foot down hard.

It kangaroo-hopped a couple of times as the engine roared. The revs were too high but as the revs dropped, the car began to ease forward more smoothly. She turned sharply to the right, the revs increased again and the Mini began to tear away.

*

A small police car slowly drew along the road and came to a silent stop outside the Cardinal's Cap.

*

The Mini, gripping every contour of the road as if it was moulded to it, raced very quickly down the narrow lane.

*

The two policemen climbed out, adjusted their hats and, after a moment to look up at the pub sign to reassure themselves that it was the right place, they slowly entered.

*

Her radio was under the control panel and she had to look down to switched it on.

*

As the policemen entered, everyone in a ripple across the pub, turned and on seeing them a hush spread quickly. The policemen looked around and noticed that dotted around there were several small groups. Ignoring any groups of women or mixed groups, the two officers approached a nearby group, but as those questioned shook their heads, the officers came deeper and deeper into the room.

One of the officers arrived at their table, where John

and Joe were sitting. Paul was heading back from the bar with his fresh pit and paused a few paces away as he saw the policeman stand beside John.

'Excuse me gentlemen, I'm sorry to trouble you, but do either of you gentlemen know a Miss Ruth Holland?'

'Yes, she's a friend. We're meeting her here later, why?'

'Sir, we need you to come with us urgently.'

Joe turned to Paul as a nervous fear gripped them both.

*

She leant forward to adjust the volume, pressing the accelerator pedal and the car began to gather more speed, approaching a sharp corner quickly, its double set of reflective chevrons flashing like a beacon in the yellowish beam of her headlamps.

She looked up, shock gripping her as with both hands on the steering wheel she tightened her hold, her knuckles turning white.

'What?!....' she cried, as instinctively her foot slammed on the brakes.

Her car began to shake and skid from side to side as it tried to stop. As the squeal of her brakes and the smell of rubber filled the air, the car shuddered and began to slide sideways across to the other side of the road.

There was a loud explosion. The car jolted and twisted violently as her left front tyre burst, sending a small cloud of rubber and steel shards rattling along the underside.

The steering wheel almost tugged itself from her grasp as she fought hard to regain control.

Slowing, but with a momentum that was still too fast for the bend, she steered into it, still on the wrong side of the road, just as a set of headlights from another car touched the beams of her lights.

Suddenly her car interior was lit up by the bright headlights. She quickly pulled the wheel instinctively to her left. Her car slewed past the other one, as it screeched to an emergency stop, and they missed each other by just a few feet.

The Mini went into a 180-degree turn and skidded off the road, past the chevrons and sideways towards a large oak tree.

She screamed and held her arms up to defend herself as the trunk of the large tree raced towards her.

Then everything turned white.

4

Ruth could feel the warmth upon her arms and the kiss of a gentle breeze on her skin. She pulled her arms away from her face and above her was a nice bright-blue sky, hardly a cloud in view and the warm sun shone large and radiant above her.

She sat up. She was on top of a high embankment, to one side a narrow country road, the other, as far as the eye could see, field after field with some woods in the distance.

It was then she noticed she was dressed in a long sleeve top, skinny jeans and battered canvas shoes without socks.

She stood and tried get her bearings. Nothing looked familiar and there didn't seem to be anywhere to go either, but there had to be somewhere. There was a road. So she decided to follow the gentle slope of the road down into the valley and began to walk for a few paces in that direction.

'I wonder where I am? How long have I been here? And where are the others?'

She stood for a moment in the centre of the road and looked along each way, thinking hard in her mind for anything that might seem familiar, but it was just some non-descript country lane, nothing remarkable about any of it.

'Oh well.' She shrugged. 'Can't stand here forever!'

She strolled on for what seemed like hours, though the sun didn't seem to move. The lane rose and fell and twisted and turned but there was no side road that joined it and, not that she gave it much thought, she didn't see another person, car or anything pass her from either direction.

As she chewed a stalk of grass, she blindly carried on in the certain knowledge that the road had to lead somewhere.

She paused and smiled.

The end of the lane opened out onto a large tarmac yard before the entrance to an old red-brick Victorian railway station. The name under the British Rail sign read, 'Halt End'.

The window frames were green, with two large green doors in the centre. There was a cream-coloured fence that ran along the sides of the building the length of the platform.

Though it looked clean, well maintained and in use, it was strangely quiet and devoid of any signs of life. However, there was a familiar red phone box with the little slatted windows a few yards down from the main entrance.

She checked her left pocket and, to her relief, her wallet was there and she had money in it. With a determined stride, she crossed the yard and entered the station.

The ticket hall was a large cavernous room. On the left halfway between entrance and platform, set flush against the oak panelling of the wall, there was a long, curve-topped window, with its slot for speaking through and little chrome cup underneath, into which the tickets and money could be exchanged. The exit to the platform was right opposite the main entrance.

There were four green, wooden benches back to back in the middle of the waiting room as well as a carousel on which there were some special break, information leaflets and there were a couple of black bins either end of the benches.

On the far wall either side of the platform entrance there was a number of large poster frames in which were all the timetables, set out for easy reading, and opposite the ticket office, up near the eaves of the ceiling, there was a large clock, white with Roman numerals in a big, green, metal case, showing the time was 11:58 as it ticked softly, the only sound she could hear apart from the gentle swinging of the door behind her.

She took a moment to look at everything before slowly walking over to the ticket office.

The blind was up and it seemed they were open for business, but after a moment she bent down a little and peered through the glass. To her surprise, the ticket office seemed abandoned.

She tapped twice on the glass.

'Hello? Anyone about?'

She waited. No one came.

She turned and looked about the waiting room once more whilst leaning on the ticket-office counter.

'Busy place, isn't it?' she sighed.

With what felt like an almighty effort, feeling for some reason a little tired, she pushed herself up and headed over to the benches. Then slowly, after patting the top of the benches as she passed them by, she made her way out onto the platform.

On the platform, she noticed how the station was well-maintained and nicely painted. Near the door there was an old, green-painted, metal chocolate dispenser, the price of 1d picked out in cream, and she thought it was cute how a redundant relic, instead of being junked, had been restored to give the station a little character.

There was no litter about that she could immediately see and all she could hear was loud ticking of the old-fashioned platform clock high above her.

The time was 11:58.

There were a number of benches at intervals along the platform and, at one end on the other side of the track, she could see a white, wooden signal box, but she couldn't see anyone in it.

She walked a little way up the platform looking at the station and at the adverts. The posters were all in a 1930's art-deco style and, much to her bemusement, they were all the same, advertising the same product. She stopped, then went over to the edge of the platform and looked down at the tracks, which she could see were nice and shiny.

'Well, at least the trains are running?!'

She turned back and, as she walked to the middle of the platform, she turned round in a full circle, looking all around.

She felt completely confused and, for the first time, she felt completely alone.

5

The large fluorescent strip light flickered momentarily as it began to fizz and then returned to a settled hum.

Paul was standing by the large, double, rectangular window looking out to the darkness and the yellow, gleaming streetlamps diffused by the white lights of the houses in the distance beyond the darkness that filled the void between.

Behind him was the bland, pale-green room with its hard plastic seats running all around the walls facing in towards two low-set coffee tables of cream Formica and chrome.

On one side sat Joe, his coat pulled around him, on the other side of the room John, his feet crossed at the ankles as he stared without any emotion at the space above the coffee tables.

There was a number of old magazines and a couple

of newspapers in untidy piles on both of the tables, but none of them felt like reading.

They were quiet and a little withdrawn, only the sound of the normal, calm hospital activities echoing along the corridor, breaking their silence.

'I suppose I should give Debbie a ring?' Paul spoke, not looking away from the window.

'Wait until we know what's going on,' John replied, still staring into space.

'I suppose you're right, only I don't want her to worry if I'm late home....'

'We know.'

The hush returned.

The door opened.

Paul looked up and in the reflection in the glass, he could see the nurse enter in her clean, pressed, pink uniform and white hat, followed by the doctor in his long white coat.

John lifted his head and stood up. The nurse half turned to the doctor. 'These are her friends, Doctor.'

'Hi, John Stanger.' John introduced himself and pointed to the others in turn. 'Paul Still and Joe Webber.'

'You're Miss Holland's friends?' the doctor asked.

'And work colleagues.' John added.

'Good.' He seemed to John to be interested and concerned. He was a similar age to Paul, not as tall, with short, black hair and a granite expression that never seemed to change as he continued, 'Then hopefully you'll be able to help us to answer some of these questions.'

'We gave your nurse, her mother's and brother's telephone numbers, but like we said, her cousin got married today and we're not sure what time any of them will be back home,' John replied, a little tiredness echoing in his voice.

'I understand that. It's only that we haven't been able to get hold of either of them and before we can operate, we need to know some things about her,' the doctor replied.

'Sure, fire away!'

'Do you know if she is on any medication for any medical conditions?'

'No. She's not on anything.' John shook his head as if to underline his reply.

'Is she allergic to antibiotics?'

'No, no, she's not.' John smiled wryly. 'She's just your typical normal girl!'

'Is she going to be alright?' Joe asked, his eyes shimmering with the glaze of tears welling up inside.

'I'm sorry, but it's too early to say at the moment.' The doctor's tone became more serious. 'I won't pretend with you. She has suffered multiple fractures to her skull and arms, not to mention losing a lot of blood from internal bleeding as well as the external cuts caused by the crash. She's lucky. She was seen to promptly, but if she is to have a chance of survival, we have to operate on her as soon as possible.'

'I see.' Joe nodded as Paul crossed to sit by him, placing a reassuring arm around his shoulder.

'But she does have a chance? Doesn't she, Doctor?' John asked.

'I promise you we will do all we can for her.' He looked at his clipboard. 'One last thing. Do you know her blood group?'

'No, sorry.' John shook his head.

'It's not one of the requirements on our forms.' Paul added.

'Okay.' The doctor continued, trying to sound more positive. 'Thank you. I know you're concerned for her but do try to relax. She's in good hands now.'

The doctor and the nurse then left, the door swinging closed behind them.

'Do you think she'll pull through?' Joe asked.

'Ruth's a strong girl. If anyone can come back from this, she can,' Paul replied as John crossed over to the window and looked out into the darkness.

As he stood there, he pinched the bridge of his nose, to hold back the tears forming in his eyes.

6

Ruth entered the waiting room again and walked slowly over to the ticket office window. She peered in but still there was nobody inside. She knocked on the window twice, waited and then knocked twice again.

'Hello?' And waited. She drummed her fingers on the counter. 'Oh, this is hopeless!' The frustration boiled up inside. She slapped the counter in anger and stormed out of the station, back outside to the road.

She'd only gone a few paces when she stopped and looked about her. No matter where she turned there were no other signs of human life. She looked over to the telephone box, a red beacon, like a lighthouse showing her the way to safety, and quickly she rushed over to it.

On the board behind the phone she could see the box's number but the address had been vandalised. She shook her head as she sighed. Just typical she thought.

Even out here nothing was safe. Then from her jeans pocket she pulled out some change.

On the black, metal shelf next to the long, grey, metal phone, she spread out her change and picked up a ten-pence piece, which she placed over the larger of the two slots below the black dial. She picked up the receiver and was about to push the ten pence into the slot when she realised that there was no dialling tone.

She depressed the connection pins twice, then twice more but there was still no dialling tone. Then with a disappointed sigh, she replaced the handset.

Gently she head-butted the top of the telephone as she tried to think what to do next, but she was confused and couldn't think of anything, her mind paralyzed by the peculiarity of the situation when, in the distance, she could hear the sound of a shrill train whistle.

Quickly, she gathered up her money and slipped it all into her pocket as she clattered though the door and, still forcing her hand out of her pocket, she ran back to the station and rushed out onto the platform. To her surprise, there was no train, only some swirling smoke wafting down from the right-hand end of the platform. It swept down and all around her, so that, for a moment, she was momentarily disorientated by the swirls of steam and smoke and in her momentum, she felt she was about to fall.

But as the smoke cleared, she was standing all alone and everything was quiet again but for the sound of the clock.

The time was 11:58.

She turned to the signal box and she could see the signal, a little further along the track, was up lighting the green glass. But as she stared at the signal box, she wasn't able to see if there was anyone there or not. Not a shadow moved behind that long wall of glass windows.

For a moment, a shiver ran down her spine. She felt she was being watched and she turned quickly, looking behind her, but she was still very much alone.

She spun around on her heels and headed back into the ticket hall.

Hands on hips and feeling more annoyed than anything else, she looked around her, but still there was no one else about, so with a sigh of resignation and with a curiosity to discover just where she was she crossed over to the nearest carousel.

The leaflets were for attractions all over Kent. Leeds Castle, Hever Castle, Dreamland, Cobham Hall, Dover Castle, Dickensian Rochester, the Whitstable Oyster Festival, Penshurst Place, the Historic Whitbread Farming Museum, Chatham Dockland Museum and Historic Chilham and its castle.

As she came around the carousel to read some more of the leaflets, she was startled momentarily by a young girl's voice.

'Excuse me.' Ruth turned to face the speaker and was surprised to see a young schoolgirl, no older than eleven.

She was wearing a grey pinafore dress, white blouse with matching knee-high socks, black, patterned leather shoes that were fastened by a side buckle, and a blazer with white piping around the sleeve ends, the hem of the blazer, the pocket tops and around the collar edges.

On the breast pocket, there was a badge of a white shield with the letters HDS in blue copperplate script forming a triangle and she had on a straw boater, tilted back on her head at such an angle that its brim was like the silhouette of a halo. The band around it was red with gold-and-blue diagonal stripes, matching her tie.

Over her shoulder and hanging to her waist was a small, brown, leather satchel and in her hands she was holding an envelope.

She was a fresh-faced girl, with a small number of freckles over the bridge of her nose and under her eyes, which were a vivid blue. Her short hair, was a light, strawberry ginger and didn't quite reach her shoulders.

'Yes?' Ruth asked.

'Letter for you,' the schoolgirl replied, offering the envelope to her.

'For me?!'

'Yes.' The schoolgirl nodded as Ruth took the letter from her and opened it.

She began to read the handwritten letter inside. At first, she was a little bemused by it, but as she read it again, she became confused. Then as she began to digest what it said, an overwhelming feeling of distress washed over her. She trembled and, looking up from the letter, she asked the girl.

'Who gave you....' She stopped and looked around the room, but the girl was gone.

Quickly she ran to the main entrance, swinging open the door, but the yard and all before her was empty. She dashed back to the platform, looking both ways, but there was no one.

She came back into the ticket hall as the realisation that she was on her own again began to dawn upon her.

No, she told herself, the schoolgirl had to have come from somewhere. She began to think hard, biting her bottom lip, trying to figure out what was going on.

7

'Can I help you?'

Ruth spun around on her heels to see the station guard standing in the platform entrance.

'Sorry?'

'Can I help you?' he asked again.

He was wearing a very smart, dark-blue, two-piece uniform, the jacket of which had a tramline of white braiding around the cuff, that turned at a right angle to the edge of the sleeve level with his little finger, and four buttons up to the collar. On the epaulets there was a small, silver-colour British Rail badge. His round cap, had matching braiding around the rim of the peak and up to the vent holes either side of the hat, with the larger logo cap badge in the centre of the front.

There were three pockets to the jacket, two normal side pockets large enough to keep items such as a ticket punch and notebooks and on the right side, a small pocket just above the larger one in which he kept his pocket watch.

He had short dark-brown hair, brown eyes and clean-shaven yet nondescript features, which made him seem indifferent to his task.

'Er... Yes, I'd like a ticket to Rochester, please?' she answered with a bright smile, her melancholy lifting at last.

'I'm sorry. I can't do that,' the guard replied.

'What?'

'I can't sell you a ticket to Rochester.'

'Right,' Ruth sighed. 'Fine. I'll have a ticket to London and I'll get a ticket to Rochester from there.' She crossed over to the ticket office window, yet to her surprise, the guard stayed where he was.

'I'm sorry, but I can't sell you any tickets.'

'Look.' She gritted her teeth angrily. 'I'm not in a mood for games, okay?! I can't find my workmates, I've just had a stupid letter from some stupid little girl and now you're telling me you can't sell me any tickets!' She rolled her eyes as she vented her frustration with a loud sigh. 'Why not?'

'Two reasons,' he replied but didn't continue as if she should already know what they were.

'What?' she asked a little blankly.

'Firstly, no trains stop here.'

'But I just heard one a moment ago!' She pointed out to the track.

'But it didn't stop.' He smiled. 'No train stops here, unless it's your destiny for it to do so, and your letter doesn't say a train will stop here, does it?'

'It might do!' she snapped defensively, gripping the letter more firmly in her grasp.

'You're going to die within the next forty-eight hours.' He smiled, continuing as if he was explaining the timetable to her. 'That is your destiny and that is why I can't sell you a ticket.'

'What do you mean?' Her head was swimming now. She couldn't comprehend what he was saying. 'I'm only twenty? I've my whole life ahead of me.'

'Obviously not.' He smiled. 'It looks like most of it's behind you.'

'But I'm too young to die!'

'You're never too young to do anything! And dying is one of those things we all have to do!' He shrugged.

'But I don't want to die!!' she exclaimed vehemently.

'We can't fight destiny.' He shrugged. 'Just because you can't have what you want, that isn't any reason to get all upset about it. Relax, enjoy your stay here. You'll be surprised just how quickly time will fly by.'

'But I don't want to stay here,' she protested. 'I should be at work. I'm an environmental scientist. I should be out there defending the environment!' She pointed out to the main entrance as if to underline her point.

'From whom?' he asked.

'From people destroying it and wiping out the planet.'

'You'll never be able to wipe out the planet.' He smirked, shaking his head as if he couldn't believe her naivety. 'It's been tried three times before with the ice ages but as long as a life form survives, the planet will evolve again.'

'But the human race....'

'You said the planet,' he reminded her, 'not the human race. Those are two different issues and if the human race wants to destroy itself just to make a few bucks, then why should I be bothered?'

'But?'

'Is there anything else I can get you?' he asked politely.

'Okay,' she conceded, trying another tack. 'If there's no train, then which way is it to the nearest village? I'll walk it if I have to!'

'To where?' he asked.

'The nearest town?'

29

'But there are no towns.'

'Then how do I leave here?'

'You don't. It's not in your destiny. You can't fight destiny.'

'But I don't want to die!' She protested almost feeling as if she would cry, but she wouldn't give him the satisfaction.

'How do you know. You haven't tried it yet!'

'But surely if a train stops?'

'But they don't,' he reminded her.

'But if they did?' she pressed him.

'You can't change your destiny,' he repeated. 'Now if you haven't got any other questions, I must get on. I've got to make sure the station remains tidy.'

She watched in disbelief as the guard then made his way back out to the platform and the door closed gently behind him. Everything was suddenly quiet again but for the soft tick of the clock high on the wall.

8

The fluorescent light hummed. John was back in his seat. Joe, his arms crossed tight against his body, was still opposite him. The room was silent as if a single sound would bring the whole world crashing down.

The door opened. They looked round and their fear subsided as Paul entered carrying a cardboard tray with cups of hot drinks from a machine slotted into three of the four holes.

He set the tray down on the coffee table and sat one seat down from John.

'They didn't have any soup so I got you a hot chocolate instead.' He set one of the cups down on the table nearer to Joe.

'Cheers,' Joe replied as he leant over and picked up his hot chocolate.

'Your tea.'

'Thank you,' John replied as Paul handed him his drink.

Paul took his own off the tray and as he sat back he asked, 'How long's it been now?'

'An hour,' John replied.

'And they still won't tell us anything!' Joe added bitterly as he looked into his cup.

'They've begun the operation,' Paul confirmed taking a sip of his drink before adding, 'I asked the nurse whilst I was getting the drinks.'

'So all we can do now is wait!' John sighed.

Joe stood. 'I can't stand this. It's driving me crazy!' he cried, the anxiety etched upon his face.

'Don't let it get to you.' John took a sip of his tea.

'Don't let it get to me?!' Joe snapped at him. 'She's only a year younger than me!! I mean, it's frightening, isn't it?!'

'Don't keep thinking about it.'

'But, I mean, if she dies, I mean,' he struggled to get his rambling mind back under control. As his fear was brought back into check, he continued, 'until tonight I never really ever thought that, you know, that I could die.' John nodded sympathetically as he understood and Joe continued, 'but when something like this happens, it makes you wonder. I mean, you can't tell, can you? I mean, when you wake up in the morning, you can't tell, can you, if you're going to make it to the end of the day, can you? I mean....'

'It's okay, Joe,' John reassured him.

'I mean.' Joe looked into his drink. The futility of it all was overwhelming. 'She doesn't deserve to die, does she?'

'Of course not,' John replied.

'Then, why is she?'

'Think positively.'

'Why? What good will that do her?!' Joe sighed.

'I don't know.' John shrugged. 'But if she thought that we were writing her off now, that we weren't there for her, then I'm sure she wouldn't fight for her life. We've got to be strong for her. We've got to or else how can we expect her to be strong for us?'

A quiet calm drifted over them as they each began to drink their drinks and after a few moments' reflection, Joe came back to his seat.

"ere.' Paul broke the silence. 'Do you remember that time when we were all working up on the River Stour, up by Wye?'

'The seeping quick-lime?' John asked.

'That's the one.' Paul smiled, remembering that day as if it was yesterday, when something funny struck him and he grinned silently.

'That was her first proper investigation, wasn't it?' John asked.

'Aha,' Paul nodded, 'and you remember that joke we played on her?'

'You asked her to get, what was it, a quick net?'

'Fast net, for use in fast-flowing water, to capture the fast-moving lime.'

'She walked all the way back to the truck before she realised we were winding her up.'

'Got you back though, didn't she?!' Joe grinned.

'Sure did.' Paul agreed.

'Gave you a sample of bog water to examine.' John laughed for a moment. 'That's right, only she forgot to tell you it came from our office toilet.'

'I spent an hour trying to figure out why the water was so sterile.' He shook his head, amazed he'd been so slow and she'd got him so easily.

For a moment they were each with their thoughts then Joe broke the silence.

'I just wish I could help.'

'Don't we all?' John replied.

9

Her car skidded a full 180 degrees. She was pushed sideways into her door while she fought with the wheel, but as the lights from the cars, the green of the grass and trees swirled like a blurred kaleidoscope pattern before her, she gritted her teeth and pushed harder on the brakes.

The squeal of the other car's tyres echoed loud in her head as her car sliced between the two chevron signs and continued to hurtle on towards a large oak tree.

She turned to see it coming closer, her arms raised to shield her as time slowed and all sound stopped.

The car smashed into the tree and as it shuddered against it, she carried on sliding sideways, meeting her door as it began to buckle inward. The side window suddenly turned all white, beginning to snow shards of tiny crystal-like fragments all over her. The rear window and the windscreen went white as they too shattered, then disintegrated, showering the entire interior space of the car with glass.

*

It all went white.
Then there was a beeping noise.
She was quiet. She was calm, only the beeping noise, only the white.

*

The nurse entered the room. Isolated in a single bed in a room all to herself, she lay there, the patient.

She was lying on her back, her face, arms and torso, heavily bandaged so that only a few wisps of her long, blonde hair were exposed between the crossover of the different bandage wraps.

She was hooked up to a drip as well as several machines by strands of wires like a rainbow web reaching across her, monitoring her breathing, her heart and brain as she lay there, motionless. The only sounds were the beep of the monitor every two seconds and the click of the rising and falling of the air pump, the tube from which was lost in the bandages that covered her face, as it forced air into her lungs.

The nurse picked up the chart at the bottom of her bed and compared the notes to the numbers on the machines. Then, after replacing it, she checked that the drip bag was still administering a steady flow of morphine to the poor girl.

Everything seemed as it should. Everything was stable.

*

Ruth held a hand to her forehead, shielding the sun

from her eyes and looked out over the yard to the road and the fields beyond. She gazed along the road to the countryside and was surprised by how isolated the station was. No farms, no villages, no towns or any industry for as far as she could see, nothing like chimney smoke or pylons in the distance.

Nothing.

She sighed heavily. It appeared there was only the one road and it had been so long from where she had started to the station in the first place, that she began to feel disheartened as she considered that, although the road might lead to some town or village somewhere, she didn't know how long it was and she might have already walked the shorter distance and, as she remembered, she'd seen no one before she reached the station.

She heard the doors swing behind her, but took no notice as the schoolgirl came over to stand beside her.

'What now? Another letter?' She snapped at her without looking at her.

'No.' The girl replied.

'What then?'

'Nothing!' The girl shrugged and for a moment she just stood there beside Ruth looking out over the fields. 'I was just wondering what it was you were thinking about. That's all!'

'I was just thinking how lonely it is out here!' Ruth admitted.

'Yes.'

Ruth sighed heavily as she slipped both her hands into her pockets.

'So.... isolated,' she began. 'I would have thought that someone else would have passed this way by now!'

'True....' the girl agreed. 'But then, isolation isn't anything new to you, is it?' she asked turning to Ruth.

'How do you mean?' She looked at the schoolgirl.

'Think about your past? When you were young?'

Ruth turned away and looked back down the road.

She began to think, to recall a sad time in her mind.

'Most of my early childhood was fine, well, as fine as anyone else's I would say... But I suppose it all started to go wrong about, I don't know, when I was eight or nine, just after my sister was born....'

10

She was standing at the end of a long corridor, no doors or windows either side, just a long straight corridor. Overhead, each just a couple of metres apart, there were several round, hard, green, plastic lampshades with white interiors and fat, round bulbs inside, from which emanated a dull, white light, breaking the corridor into patches of light and shade.

She wanted to walk forward, but she couldn't. She kicked off her shoes and barefoot, she ran, through light and dark, light and dark. She ran with all her strength towards a bright, shimmering light at the far end of the corridor, the light flickering to shade and then back to light again, until she slowed and stopped when she reached the end of the corridor.

A tall, black, double gothic-style, iron gate stood before her as swirling clouds of mist filtered through the rails and sank down to form a mist about her bare feet.

She took hold of the gates, pushing down the latch and was about to enter when she noticed the numbers on the two gates. On the left it read 11, on the right 33. Then she pushed them apart and rushed forward into the mist.

For a moment the light was bright and she had to shield her eyes. Then as she opened them, she was aware she was outside.

A silvery-grey mist clung to the ground, cold around her ankles, as if it was a blanket of ice vapour covering all the land, drifting in between the grass and headstones.

Ruth stood alone, dressed in a long, black dress and a black hat with a veil, holding in her black-lace gloved hands, a bouquet of black and red tulips.

Before her, spread inside a white box of edging stones, was a sea of loose, turquoise stone chippings that rippled away from her to the headstone at the far end.

She looked at it. The inscription read 'To a Late and Lamented Father.'

*

'...I suppose the changes were hardest on me, being the middle child of three. My brother was old enough to understand what was going on and my sister was too young to notice anything outside her play-pen. But I noticed....'

*

She began to drop each flower onto the grave, one after the other, black then red, then black and so forth.

*

'At first it had been the odd late night, then the rows. Then my father began to forget things... like my birthday and things like that. He even forgot to buy us a turkey for Christmas once.'

*

She smelt a red tulip and then let it fall onto the chippings before her.

*

'We ended up eating soup and sausages, and, I mean, it's not as though Christmas isn't well-signposted in advance!'

*

She paused for a moment, four flowers left, she looked at them and with a gentle smile she let them fall from her hands onto the grave. Then, without any more reverence, she turned and walked away, down the tarmac path, deeper into the darker, tree-lined avenue of larger, taller monuments. As the mist began to rise and blow between these larger memorials, she kept her head down and walked on down the path with quick, small steps.

*

'I suppose I could have gone one of two ways. As a teen, I could have turned into a real wild child, staying out all night, drinking, taking drugs, sleeping around, anything to find a replacement for the warm loving relationship I was losing from my family life. But even though I'm not religious, I did have a higher moral standard for myself, probably more so than most religious people and I certainly found it extremely easy to adhere to, which can't be said for most devout people who seem to digress from their beliefs most religiously. So I became quiet and introverted, kept myself to myself and worked for what I wanted most. A good settled life.'

∗

The monuments got larger, some with full human-sized angels, one of a horse with its head bowed. She walked by, not stopping to read or look at them, but as she came round a bend, she stopped by a statue of a naked Adam and Eve, entwined in a lovers' kiss.

Ivy was growing around the plinth on which they stood and the stone had been aged by the weather and the lichens, but the detail, their love, was still clearly etched beautifully into the stone.

She turned away, looking down to the ground, and closed her eyes.

∗

'However, it wasn't long before his discreet alcoholism became an obvious one, as his once handsome features became haggard and blotched and before long his promising career and our privileged lifestyle became eroded to little more than a collection of vodka bottles and welfare giros. Two days before my thirteenth birthday he left the house never to return and, just after my fifteenth, his live-in lover rang to tell us he had died of liver failure, a most heroic end to the most pathetic of losers.'

She could hear some ticking, some fast, some a double beat, some high-pitched, others low and slow. She looked up and she found herself standing on a narrow path, with the mist swirling around the tall monuments hemming her in and a funeral procession slowly marching towards her. They were all dressed in black and she stared at them, aghast, as she saw that each person's face had been replaced with a clock, and the ticking she could hear was coming from each face.

Some of them were a ring of numbers, with two hands, some had the second hands, others were digital, some were even made of a row of tiles that flipped over when the minutes or hours changed. But all were showing the same time, 11:58.

She turned to look back along the path. There with the mist swirling thick behind her, the schoolgirl stood smiling. Ruth ran towards her but the schoolgirl turned and slipped between two of the monuments into a cloud of mist and was gone.

Ruth darted between the stones, her bare feet, slipping on the grass as she ran. She rounded a huge monument and down a little path to the lichgate. She was running so hard she almost ran into the gate. Leaning on it, she gripped the top so tightly, as if she was trying to sink her claws into it, before she took a deep, calming breath and passed through, letting the gate slam shut behind her.

She was dressed in her long-sleeved top and jeans once more, walking barefoot through a hard, tarmac schoolyard, where a large number of secondary schoolchildren where letting off steam between the previous and the next lessons, each and every one of them oblivious to Ruth as she slowly went further and further into the yard.

*

'It was during that time that I threw myself into my work. I studied all the sciences and gained the reputation of being a swot. I wouldn't say I was really withdrawn, just quiet. Yet, it didn't stop the bullying. But when your father's an alcoholic, it doesn't seem so much fun anymore, to be out there behind the bike sheds, downing cheap cider and smoking cigarettes just because Alice Buckley, the school bike does it! I knew if I was to better myself, I could not just regain the self-respect my father had eroded

from me over those years, but I also had to do some good.
I could see life from both aspects and, when I had my own
family, I would do all I could to ensure that they only
knew the good, the right way to live. After all, it's easy to
be happy, but so many people just like living a lie and end
up making themselves and anyone they can feel sad.'

*

In front of her, a small group of boys parted out of
Ruth's way to reveal the schoolgirl, holding in her hand a
long-stemmed glass of red wine. She smiled as her eyes
met Ruth's and, as she looked away, the girl dropped the
glass.
The glass tumbled, the wine began to spill and when
the glass hit the cold, grey tarmac, it shattered and the wine
inside splashed out in all directions.
The wine splattered her bare feet.
The girl looked up.
'And are you happy now?

11

Ruth looked down at her battered canvas shoes then out over the road and the fields once more. She sighed, then turned to the schoolgirl who was still standing beside her.

'Of course!'

'Even though you're a social inadequate?!' the schoolgirl asked.

'What?'

'I would have thought someone who couldn't relate to anyone would be glad they were going to die?'

'I can relate to others. I just wanted to better myself. That's all.' Ruth defended herself, feeling more than a little insulted.

'What for?' the girl asked.

'So I could have a really good life and also so I could help save the planet.'

'Who said the planet was in danger?' the schoolgirl asked curiously.

'All the pollution and the devastation of the rain forests for one!'

'But you could wipe out all but one amoeba from this planet and in about 100 million years you'd be back to square one!' The girl indicated around the railway station yard, to the fields and beyond.

'But if we don't do something to protect our environment, we'll destroy the human race!'

'Oh, that. Well, does it really matter?'

'What?'

'Does it really matter? I mean, you're all going to die out some day. Better to make it sooner rather than later.'

Ruth was disappointed that the girl saw no future for anyone, not even herself.

'But we don't have to become extinct?!'

'It is the destiny of all things to die. You can't change your destiny. As you will find out in just over two days' time. I mean, look up at the stars at night and hold this thought. In the heavens there are billions of stars in an ever-expanding universe, of which your planet is a speck of dust on which, like on countless of billions of other specks of dust, the accident of life is occurring. Why should your life or that of anyone else's be any more significant? Nothing you do now or in the future will alter the progress of this planet or its eventual death, so why are you clinging on to something so pointless and worthless?'

'Life must be worth something?'

'Possibly.' The schoolgirl shrugged. 'But only if what gives it a purpose gives it a value, makes it worth having and if you're without worth in this world then what can be the point of remaining?'

Ruth rounded on her angrily.

'Shouldn't you be at school!' Then Ruth turned away, looking back down the road.

'You can't change your destiny!'

'Of course I can. I could leave here.'

'How?' The schoolgirl asked curiously.

'By going down this road.'

'Where to?'

'To the nearest village. There has to be one somewhere, because there's a train track running in and out of this place!'

The schoolgirl grinned.

'But you can't leave here. It is your destiny to stay. You can't go. There is nowhere to go!'

'Just stop me.'

She began to run. Like a greyhound out of the traps, she ran down the road and round the sweeping corner.

The schoolgirl watched, holding the strap of her satchel and smiled.

Her lungs felt like they were going to burst and already she was feeling the lactic burn in her calf muscles slowing her down. All she could hear was the sound of her own laboured breath and, as she slowed and came to a gentle rest, she turned back to the corner.

A weak smile came to her lips as she puffed hard through her flushed cheeks. The railway station was no longer in view, but more to her relief, no one, no schoolgirl or station guard was following her.

'A weird bunch of freaks. No wonder no one uses the station.'

She turned away and, at a more gentle jog, she continued along the road to the next bend.

But as she rounded it, she stopped, icy cold fear running down her spine. There before her was the yard and the station, with the schoolgirl standing there, one hand holding the strap of her satchel.

She was too tired to carry on. As she began to walk back across the yard, all breathless and sweating, the schoolgirl smiled beguilingly at her. Ruth glared at her, giving her best 'drop dead bitch' look before she continued into the ticket hall.

12

Joe looked at his watch. The hum of the light was a little quieter now and it flickered twice.

'My turn, I suppose!' He looked up across the tables to the other two.

'Eh?' John replied, shaking himself from his personal thoughts.

'Another drink?' Joe stood.

'Please.' John nodded.

'We should give her mother another ring,' Paul added, as he stayed staring at his shoes.

'She is still probably at the reception or staying the night.' John replied. 'Ruth only left early because she was coming to see us.'

'What about Simon?' Joe asked. 'Do you think he should know?'

John looked away uneasily as Paul replied with a little

nod. 'I'll ring him in a minute. You just get the tea.'

'Okay.'

Joe headed out. Paul watched and waited until the door closed before he turned to John.

'Do we have to ring him?' John asked without looking round.

'Look, he's her ex. He has a right to know!'

'But he never cared for her....'

'....That's not fair!'

'Well,' John conceded reluctantly, 'not completely, only in as much as it suited him. He didn't care otherwise.' He wanted to say more, but somehow he couldn't.

'I know what you're saying....' Paul replied sympathetically. 'We all touch, I suppose, once or twice in our lives, a deep feeling for someone, who if we're honest with ourselves and are lucky as well, will make us happy for all our lives, but, just because you're in pain now, don't let what's gone by hinder what has yet to come, eh?'

'But then you're the lucky one, pal. When you met Debs....'

'.... Yes, I was,' Paul agreed warmly. 'But don't spoil what you've had, mate. It's not worth destroying it for what remains!'

The waiting room door flew open and as they turned, in came Joe, carrying a tray with three paper cups steaming away.

'I got the same again, alright?' he asked, letting the door swing shut behind him.

'Sure,' Paul agreed. 'I'll give Simon a ring.'

Paul slowly rose to his feet as Joe, reaching the nearest table and setting down the tray, began to place the new cups next to the double set of empty used ones. The door opened again.

They turned expectantly to the young nurse as she entered.

'Any news?' Paul asked.

'She should be coming out of theatre in about half an

hour,' she replied with the sort of confidence that suggested she knew what was going on. They took it with the belief she did, even though in their heart of hearts, they understood she knew as much about what was really going on as they did, but they took the comfort from it as was intended. The nurse then asked, 'I really just came in to see if you were all alright, and if I could get you anything, like a blanket or a pillow each?'

'No thank you,' John smiled meekly, 'I'm fine.'

Joe shrugged.

'No, we're all just fine.' Paul replied. 'Thank you all the same.'

The nurse smiled and left.

Paul looked at the other two and then his drink. The steam was still rising like smoke from a burning tower block, far too hot to drink. The water in that machine was scalding and he was surprised none of them were now patients getting treatment for burnt tongues. It could wait. Patting the change in his pocket, he pointed to the door.

'I'll go and make that call.'

13

Everything was quiet and still. She felt quite calm and everything seemed dark. Somewhere there was this dull, constant ticking noise she couldn't shift from her mind. All her senses seemed dulled. She couldn't move. She didn't want to move. No, she couldn't move.

She could only breathe and listen to that damn dull ticking.

Suddenly she was bathed in a sweeping bright light. It stopped moving, staying on her, bright, so bright, she couldn't see anything around her. It was like the dark before it and still that annoying ticking sound continued.

Into the light moved two silhouettes, one of a man wearing some kind of cap, the other, a child, a young girl, also wearing a large brimmed hat that was like a black halo around her head in the silhouette.

For a moment the two shadows stood there, not

moving.

That ticking.

'Hello? Are you alright?' the man's voice called.

That ticking.

'Are you okay?' The girl's voice trembled with fear as she called.

What was that ticking?

'Stay up here. I'm going to take a look,' the man said.

'Okay, Daddy,' the girl replied nervously.

The man's silhouette started to come closer until everything was almost black again.

The car door opened but still all she could see was the shadow leaning over her.

'Oh my God!' he whispered.

He turned. The light returned and then everything went black. He began to scramble up the bank, his shadow receding, to become a silhouette.

The girl's voice called. 'How is she, Daddy?'

'I must phone for an ambulance, I... I,' he stammered, 'she's alive. You'd better... No, wait.'

*

Suddenly the whole world went white.

*

There was a twitch under the bandaged arm, a slight move of the head, but that was all. The monitor's pace began to slow down. All the displays began to drop slightly. She was getting weaker and the nurse watching over her took an ampoule and a syringe from a tray on a trolley by the bed. Quickly, she filled it to the desired mark and injected some adrenaline into the arm.

*

She was standing on the platform, looking down the track. It was quiet but for the sound of the clock above her and everywhere around her was deserted.

The time was 11:58.

She looked around her before she made her way over to a seat down by the corner of the platform and as she sat, she took from her jeans' back pocket a creased letter, which she began to open out and read.

As she did so she began to cry, as her emotions started to take over, the frustration and the sense of lonely isolation wearing her down as she crumpled the letter in her hands and dropped it to the floor, burying her head into her hands.

'Why all the tears?'

She looked round and a wave of uncontrollable joy began to sweep over her as there stood John, Paul and Joe.

'You're here!' she exclaimed with surprise.

'We wouldn't miss this for the world!' John replied with a cheeky grin.

*

The nurse removed the syringe, as the monitor's rhythm began to pick up to a steadier beat.

14

John looked at the tea in his paper cup. They called it tea, but he wasn't sure if it was because it was a paper cup, or because it was some instant ready mix that was flavoured to taste and smell like tea or if it really was tea. It was warm and the taste wasn't unpleasant, only it wasn't like any tea he'd ever drunk before.

He watched the brown liquid reflecting part of the fluorescent light above, still not wishing to look away from it, as if to do so would be to break the spell, wake him up and he'd discover they weren't having a dream.

The waiting room door opened as Paul returned. John watched him as he slowly joined them and when he had sat down, Joe asked. 'Did you get through?'

'I tried her mother's again, but no joy,' Paul replied, picking up his drink.

'Said they'd be staying over,' John reminded him.

'And I spoke to Simon,' Paul added. John bristled slightly.

'And?'

'He thanked me for the call, but he's not coming over. Like he said, it's all over, but he wishes her well and might send some flowers or something for when she comes round.'

John felt a bit relieved. One less awkward moment to come.

'So it's just us rooting for her then?' Joe added and finished his drink, crushing the cup slightly as he placed it down with the other dead cups on the coffee table.

*

The railway station café was bright and airy with its high, white walls and its scattering of small round tables, each with a hard white Formica top and in the centre, a small, hard, plastic container divided into compartments in which were sachets of sugar, salt, vinegar, various types of ketchups and paper napkins, a bright-red tin ashtray beside it.

Each table had an even number of seats set out to give each position the same amount of room. At the far end, opposite the other short wall and at 90 degrees to the platform, was the long counter that was almost the width of the room, chrome-fronted with a large, glass-fronted, sneeze-guard display on top, running a quarter the length of the counter at the opposite end to the till, displaying the fresh cakes and savoury items.

Between them there were two red plastic baskets. The one nearer the till had a number of individually wrapped biscuits, the other similarly wrapped sticky cakes. Behind the counter on the back wall there was another surface on which sat the tea and coffee makers and the microwave and was the preparation area for anyone who wanted any of the hot options marked up on the old-fashioned, chalk-style display on the wall above. The counter and the rear surface ended by the door opposite the till to the staff-room and store.

There was a chilled cabinet down by the end where the sneeze guard was, in which the hot options were kept cold prior to microwaving and apart from the normal pies, sausages and fish and chips, there were a couple of exotic options, a lasagne and curry, on the menu.

On top of the sneeze guard there was a long, blue basket in which was a selection of crisp packets, between several freshly made sandwiches wrapped in hard see-through cellophane triangular packages on their ends.

High on the wall opposite the counter a red-framed clock showed the time. It read 11:33.

Joe, Paul, John and Ruth were sitting around one of the tables, near the door, by the window overlooking the platform. They each had a hot drink, and Joe was eating a bag of crisps whilst John examined the letter.

After taking a sip, Paul placed his cup down on its saucer and, turning to Ruth, asked, 'And you have no idea where this place is?'

'I can't even find a map! It's like it's right out in the sticks somewhere,' she replied. 'I mean, there's lots of fields and plants and countryside and so on about the place. But wherever you turn, you just see greenery. There's not a house, pylon, or telegraph pole to be seen anywhere!'

'Suppose you've looked for the Land Rover?'

'Wouldn't know in which direction to go now.'

'What's the station like?' Joe asked through a mouthful of smokey bacon.

'Just a normal station!' she shrugged. 'That's why it's so bizarre.'

'Well.' John folded the letter back in half. 'It's blunt and to the point.'

He gave the letter back to her. Paul held out his hand to take it and she passed it to him. As he opened it out to read, she replied, 'I know. I found it all a bit distressing.'

'I'm not surprised!' John agreed.

Joe screwed up his empty crisp packet and dumped it in the ashtray.

'The problem is I think they mean it!' she added, the nervousness echoing in her voice. Paul finished reading the letter and asked, 'But why would anyone want to kill you?'

'Don't know.' She shrugged. 'It's all a mystery to me!'

John took the letter and started to read it again.

'But then this whole place is strange,' Joe agreed.

'You're telling me!' she sighed.

'We'll just have to get away from here, that's all,' John added as he handed the letter back to her again.

'How?' She struggled not to stand as she forced the letter back into her jeans' back pocket. 'I've tried running away!'

'What about the train?' Paul asked.

'That must leave here?' John echoed as Ruth smiled wryly to them both.

'Well, I know it runs through here, the tracks are silvery, but it doesn't stop.'

'Then that has to be the answer!' John replied.

'But how can we stop it?' she asked. 'There are no accurate time tables up, no leaflets, no announcements.'

'Yeah,' Joe frowned, 'and I noticed that the time on the clocks doesn't change.'

'Which all seems to prove that the answer to our problems is in stopping a train.' John underlined his conclusion with a glance out to the platform.

'True,' Paul agreed with a nod. 'They've certainly gone to some lengths to stop us from knowing when the next one is coming.'

'Well, apart from the counter assistant here, there's only the guard and that schoolgirl about the place.'

'And they can't be in more than one place at any one time so they've hidden all the information from us.' John smiled as he felt the advantage had to be theirs now.

'You've got to be careful though,' she warned him.

'How come?'

Joe stood.

'That schoolgirl is devious. I don't know, but if it wasn't for the fact she's so young, I'd say she was running this place!'

'I see?'

'Anyone want anything?' Joe asked.

'You're not still hungry, are you?' John asked as he turned to him.

'It's a long walk!' Joe defended himself, his eyes drawn to the cake display.

'No, we don't,' Paul replied. Joe peered over to the counter. 'Only I thought, I'd have a doughnut.'

'You'll turn into a doughnut one day!' John quipped with a heavy sigh.

'So you don't want one?' he asked the group again.

'No.' John shook his head.

'Ruth?' Joe turned to her.

'No, thanks. I'm watching my figure.'

'What figure. You're a matchstick!' he sighed.

'Joe.' John nodded backwards to the counter. 'Buy your cake!'

As he approached the counter, the middle-aged woman emerged from the back room and greeted him with a warm, cheery smile.

'So what are we going to do?' Ruth asked in a slight whisper.

'Stop that train, of course,' John quietly replied. 'There must be a timetable somewhere, or something that will let us know when the next one is due. When we have that, then we can work out our plan of attack!'

'Sounds good to me,' Paul agreed.

'Where shall we look?' she asked as Joe returned with his doughnut.

'I think we should split up,' John suggested

'Good idea.' Joe fumbled with the cellophane

wrapping. 'Why?'

'To find a proper timetable,' Paul sighed.

'Why split up?' Joe asked as the film came undone.

'Because two can't watch four all the time, can they?' John answered curtly.

'Ah.' Joe understood.

'Chances are that schoolgirl will find me,' Ruth snapped bitterly. 'She seems to enjoy making my life a misery.'

'Well, at least that will be one of them out of the way!' John replied, gently touching her on the hand for reassurance. 'Don't worry, okay. It won't be long now.'

She smiled affectionately as, after a brief moment, he slipped his hand away and cradled his drink just as Joe stood again.

'Where you going?' John asked.

'To have a look around,' Joe replied.

'In a mo. Finish your cake first.'

Paul finished his drink and as he placed his cup on his saucer he added, 'I'll go first. I'll check the other side of the track.'

Joe began to eat his doughnut, chewing as quickly as he could.

'Okay.' John nodded his agreement. Ruth finished her drink and watched Paul leave.

John could see the pain and the worry on her face.

'Okay?' he asked, wishing he could take the pain away.

'I'll be fine.' She smiled, but she didn't believe it.

15

Ruth entered the ticket hall and after a quick look around to see the room was empty, she crossed to the ticket-office window and peered in.

No one inside, as usual. An ironic smile crept over her lips as she told herself she shouldn't have expected anything else. She turned and she almost died of fright as standing just a yard or two away from her was the schoolgirl, grinning at her like a Cheshire cat.

'Startle you, did I?' the girl asked mockingly.

'I'm not used to people creeping up on me, that's all!'

'Me! Creeping up on you! This is a public place.'

'Without very much public,' Ruth reminded her tersely.

'All the same, I have as much right to walk here as you do.'

'Suppose.'

'And anyway,' the schoolgirl continued, 'if you're looking for the guard, he'll be doing his rounds about the station. He always does them at this time of day.'

She glanced up at the clock. It read 11:33.

'I see.'

There was an uneasy calm between them. She could feel the schoolgirl's eyes burning into her, as if she was being examined under a microscope.

Quickly she pushed past the girl, heading back towards the platform, when the girl called.

'You don't like being alone for too long, do you?'

She turned back.

'Not with you anyway!' she snapped back angrily as she fought off the desire to knock that straw boater off her head.

'Always been a little frightened of strangers, haven't you?' the schoolgirl asked.

'Aren't we all?'

'Always expect to be judged, don't you? Never feel you're ever quite worth the bother?'

'That's not fair!' Ruth cried vehemently. 'I... I get nervous about things I don't understand, but, that's only natural. I proved though that I could overcome my fears. I had to, to get my job at the Environment Office.'

16

'I had already passed the interview and had been assigned to the Medway Valley Unit. Traffic had been horrendous, but I had still managed to make it on time.'

*

Ruth nervously knocked on the door and, after taking a steadying deep breath, she entered the lab.

Immediately as she opened the door, two desks back, she saw Paul, sitting on a stool looking at a slide through his microscope, and John, a desk over, writing a report, which he stopped doing and, flicking his pen in his hand, he looked up at her.

Behind him and at the far corner of the room was Joe, washing out a small number of air-tight sealing jars with a bottle brush.

The room was wider than it was long from where she stood in the doorway, nervously smiling. She noticed the room was painted a dull lime green, with three rows of two desks and a row of workbenches under the wide rectangular windows that ran along the left-hand wall and the far wall. Between the sinks and the fourth wall there was a number of cabinets and under the workbenches by the windows all the space had been taken up by cupboards, which were the same dark-oak, stained wood as the desks.

The windows were all covered with horizontal venetian blinds, partly open so that, between the slats, she could see the car park with its boundary hedgerows and small saplings that edged the ends of each row of parking bays.

There were charts and environmental information posters, hung at regular intervals around the room. She felt they were more likely to be there to break the monotony of the green walls, as the room, with its sunken squares of fluorescent light, breaking at regular intervals the constant lines of grey polystyrene tiles, felt flat and lifeless in that sort of progressive way modern architecture aspired to these days.

'Good morning there, are you Ruth?' John asked in a neutral voice as if he wasn't sure if she was someone he should have known or not.

'Ruth Holland.' She smiled as she bobbed slightly, hesitating if she should come in or not. 'I'm, er, the new lab assistant?'

'Oh, yes.' He put his pen down. 'We're expecting you.'

He clambered off his stool and came over to her as Joe looked round to see what was going on, stopping what he was doing.

'Hello.' She held out her hand and shook his as John explained.

'John Stanger. I'm the senior scientist of this division dedicated to the survival of rural Kent, and these are my partners in crime, Paul Still.....'

'Hi.' She waved to him, as Paul, without looking away from his slide, waved back.

'....and Joe Webber.' John pointed to Joe, who grinned and called out.

'Hi.' She replied as he went back to washing out the jars.

'Not a large team, but a dedicated one, or at least we do what we can.'

She was feeling a little calmer. Her butterflies were subsiding and her worst fears about the group being too aloof or stuffy hadn't materialized. She was beginning to feel she might just fit in.

'Right.' She nodded and he then asked, 'Tea?'

She began to panic, almost flustered, and stammered.

'Er.... Okay.... er.... Where's the kettle?'

'No, sorry. I didn't make myself clear, did I?' He encouraged her to come more into the lab. She followed, not sure what was going to happen next. 'We're a team here, okay? You do your job and I don't get angry. You make a cup of tea when you want, and when you're making one, you, through the kindness of your heart and for the love of your team mates, ask the assembled rabble if they want too, okay? First lesson of the day, we're all equal here, even though I'm more equal than the rest of you. The only whipping boy in this group is the dissected mouse we've got in the chiller cabinet, so I'll ask you again. Tea?'

'Er... Yes, please, white, no sugar.'

'Good.' He smiled and she felt at ease. 'And if you can survive all that okay then you'll fit in with the gang perfectly.'

She relaxed as Paul left his desk and came over to her while John crossed to a small kettle with a number of old cups upturned on a tray, the other side of Joe and the sink.

'Good job you like tea,' Paul remarked dryly. 'We've run out of coffee.'

'I see,' she replied sympathetically.

'Anyway, here's your desk.'

He pointed to one nearest the door.

'Have you got anything for me to do?' she asked as he showed her the rack behind the door for her to hang her coat.

'You can help Joe get the kit bags ready,' John called out. 'It looks as if we'll have to take some more samples from Tobin's Farm.'

Joe shook out the last jar and placed it on the draining board as he turned off the tap.

'I'm on it.' Then he dried his hands as Ruth watched John make the four teas.

*

'It may have been unorthodox, but he made me instantly feel as though I had always been there and because of that all my nerves were gone and from then on, since I've been with the guys, I've never felt alone.'

17

The ticket-hall clock ticked on monotonously through the silence, as Ruth stared angrily into the schoolgirl's eyes.

'So they like you,' the girl sneered. 'They have to. They work with you, but it's still never close, is it?'

'I don't know what you mean!' Ruth snapped back.

'It's not like having a loving relationship,' the girl teased, playing with the strap of her satchel. 'I mean, you never stop working, do you? You're always on the go to a point where you exclude everybody else!'

'No, I don't!' She was angry at the accusation, but it still stung with a ring of truth.

'Don't you?'

'No!'

'What about your time with Simon?' the schoolgirl asked bluntly.

'That's not fair!'

'Isn't it?' The girl smirked knowingly.

'No.'

'You could never devote all your time to him, could you? Always had to hide behind the shroud you call your job!'

*

'Even when it was supposed to be special.' The schoolgirl's voice echoed in her head.

*

There were bluebells as far as the eye could see, a sea of blue, like a swathe of cloth laid over the landscape, lapping round every tree. Through the dense canopy of new leaf, the dappled light sparkled though, illuminating in part the carpet of blue. With the ripple of the gentle spring breeze, the whole mass of bluebells shimmered and seemed to dance to some silent symphony.

It was warm, but she still needed her thin coat. It was dry underfoot, but she was wearing her ankle boots just in case and she was relaxed and enjoying the effort of doing absolutely nothing, snuggled arm in arm with her much beloved Simon.

He was a couple of years older. They'd met at university, though he had been studying computer science and had the look of a technology obsessive about him. They'd first seen each other in the refectory one breakfast time, queuing up for their free boxes of cereal and cartons of milk to take back to their rooms.

After a few weeks of meeting like that, they had got chatting and after a few more weeks, they'd met at the university bar. A few weeks more and a few more pubs in town and soon they were queuing up for their boxes of cereal and cartons of milk together and deciding just whose room they should be sharing them in.

He was a little taller than her, with wavy brown hair and blue-grey eyes and the rugged good looks of a film star, just without the money. As they sauntered along the path through the carpet of bluebells, the chatter of the birds in the branches always, it seemed, some way off in the distance, everything it seemed to her was going to be like this day for the rest of her life.

'Nice pub that,' he remarked after they had walked for a while. She murmured her agreement, though she wasn't an authority on British pubs.

'We should have lunch by the river more often.'

They gave each other a hug and continued on their way.

'I love the countryside, don't you?' she asked and he made a sound which suggested he agreed. 'I love listening to the birds.'

'I like Rochester though,' he admitted.

'Where we live, and the old town.'

'True. Like any city really.'

'And I do like climbing up to the top of the castle. Even with all those stairs!'

He gave her a gentle hug. They slowed as they reached a bend in the path.

'Ruth?'

'Yes?'

'I was thinking, you know, about us?'

They stopped and turned to look at each other. He gently held her around the waist.

'What?' she asked, looking for a clue in his eyes.

'I was thinking, well, I was wondering, I mean, don't you think it's time we started living together?'

She smiled coyly.

'I... I don't know what to....' It was then that she noticed something behind him and he could tell he didn't have her attention anymore.

'What is it?' he asked, glancing back but he couldn't see anything.

'That tree, it's leaves are black.' She broke away from him as he watched her head over to the tree.

'What?' he asked again, a frustration hung in the tone of his voice as she ignored him and examined the lowest hanging branch of the tree.

'It's leaves are black, as though it's been poisoned,' She couldn't tell how and she would have to do some tests but her first impression was, 'by acid, probably.' She'd heard there had been acid rain blown in from Germany in recent years, but this damage seemed to be the result of something more ferocious, but she didn't know enough about ash trees to know what it could be.

'Ruth, it's Saturday?' he pleaded.

'But the tree?' She showed the branch to him.

'You're not at work now?!'

'Does that matter?' she asked more angrily than she had intended. 'I'm paid to look after the environment! And this could mean it's under threat. The world's dangers don't just stop, you know, because it's my bloody day off!'

'Why do you have to ruin it, Ruth! It's been such a lovely day!'

'It still is. I'll give John a ring and he'll deal with it.'

'But we don't have a phone?'

'At the pub,' she insisted.

He sighed as he rolled his eyes and thrust his hands firmly and defiantly into his pocket.

'Do you have to?'

'Yes,' she replied.

He gritted his teeth. Inside he was angry with her, but he was determined not to show it.

'But why?'

'Because it's what I do!' she replied.

18

The schoolgirl moved to Ruth's other side, her plastic heels echoing across the ticket hall.

'Believe me now?' she asked.

'Didn't stop him moving in with me,' Ruth replied. 'I remember that everything was fine.'

'You sure?' the girl taunted her.

*

The monitor began to slow and show a weakening signal. The nurse was concerned so she pressed a button on the cord above the girl's bandaged head and checked the monitor again.

*

'Yes.... We had fun, like any loving couple does!'

*

The kitchen was small. It was as wide as the lounge, with all the maple-laminated cupboards above and below the worktops that ran either side of the cooker against the dividing wall shared with the neighbouring property.

The worktop stopped before it reached either side wall as on one side was the tall, standing, slim fridge-freezer and the other side, the sink. Both the small walls had a window looking out, the sink side to the gardens of the flats opposite and the other to the main road and shops across the street.

The wall on the lounge side had a couple of rails of hooks on which were hung the cooking utensils and by the door there was a number of saucepans on a pyramid stand.

Ruth was by the sink washing up some dinner plates as Simon dried them and then placed them on a shelf in a lower cupboard next to the cooker. They both had a glass of red wine on the worktop and in-between each plate as they took their time, they sipped their wine.

Simon put a plate away and as he stopped to pick up his glass, he glanced at his watch.

'Come on, hurry up.'

'Why?' She asked looking round.

'Football's on telly in a mo!' He sipped his wine.

'And what about our early night?'

'Sorry, lover. Chelsea first always.'

She took a handful of soapy bubbles and dolloped some on the end of his nose.

'Ah, yes, yes, very mature that is!' She giggled as he put his glass down and begun to wipe them off, adding curtly. 'Yeah, like, that's a logical arguments, bubbles over football.'

She put her arms around him and, as she stared into his eyes, his attitude softened and they began to kiss.

'How's that?' she asked.

'Hum, I'm not sure, I might need a little more persuading?'

They kissed a little more passionately and held it for a little longer.

'And now?'

'I suppose I could video it!'

She gently slapped him on the arm as warm smiles crept across their lips, their minds filling with erotic thoughts. They kissed and began to put their arms around each other and forgot about the washing up.

*

The monitor's signal began to speed up as the vital signs began to show a stronger response.

The nurse was relieved.

*

The clock in the ticket hall echoed as Ruth stood silently watching the schoolgirl, suspicious of her next taunt. The girl smiled cynically as she asked, 'But wasn't it not long after that, the doubts set in?'

'You mean when Simon went for his promotion?'

*

The bedroom was decorated with a white ceiling and walls and a bright red carpet. The pine bed faced the window with its silver horizontal Venetian blinds and on the far wall away from the door there was a fitted wardrobe.

Over the bed there was large black-and-white Louise Brooks photo printed on canvas and on the wall adjacent to the door there was a large print of Roy Lichtenstein's Drowning Girl.

Either side of the bed, there was a matching pine bedside cabinet. On the one nearest the door, on Simon's side, there was a small lamp and a digital-display alarm clock and radio. On the other side, there was a lamp and a well-thumbed book, A Brave New World by Aldous Huxley.

She wiped the hair from her eyes as she rolled onto her side to look at him.

The orange light from the nearby streetlamp was creeping in under the blinds, making a zebra pattern over their red duvet.

She breathed softly watching him lie there. His eyes flickered and she could see he was still awake.

'So when will you know?' she asked.

He sighed and turned his head to her. She could see the whites of his eyes in the half-light of the room.

'In four weeks... Well, that's when they'll interview the shortlist. It'll be two months after that before I'll know if I've got it!'

'But Wales!' She still couldn't understand why he had applied for a job so far away.

'I know....' Was all he could say.

'It's a long way to commute!'

'I wasn't thinking about commuting.'

'Live there?' she asked as suddenly a cold shiver of realisation trembled down her spine.

He responded, 'People do!' It wasn't what she wanted to hear. 'And computers are a growing industry.'

'But I'm based here,' she replied.

'Couldn't you get a transfer?'

'I don't know.' She looked past him. She didn't want to know.

'Anyway, we're jumping the gun at the moment, aren't we? I mean, I haven't got the job yet!'

'I know.'

'I thought you would have been happy for me.' He felt slighted she hadn't been enthusiastic to move, or understood what a great opportunity this was for him. 'What with me having being nominated and all.'

'I am!'

'You don't sound it?'

'I am.' She tried to reassure him. 'I am truly. It's just, it's so much to take in. I mean, I've got my new job, you've moved in and we're already thinking of moving to Wales!'

'These are exciting times.' He leant over and kissed her gently on the cheek. 'Anyway, like I said it's all up in the air at the moment. Probably won't come to anything anyway!'

He snuggled back down as she rolled onto her back.

'Night.'

'Yeah.' She watched the shadows in the aertex. 'Good night.' She then rolled over, away from him.

19

The monitor began to slow, the signal weakening.

*

She sighed. Her breath seemed to echo around the ticket hall.

'I admit that I felt uneasy about the idea. I mean, I was forging my own career as it was. I was happy for him, but why should I give up something that I love for him anyway? He could have stayed where he was! We didn't need the money or anything. I mean, we were well off!'

'Because you couldn't keep a relationship. You're useless!' the schoolgirl replied.

*

The long branches of the willow trees twitched tantalisingly short of the river, desperate to touch the cool, crystal, water flowing fast beneath them and yet unable to.

In the long grass, which was bent to the river bank by the wind echoing the shape of the tree, Ruth and John were sat with their packed lunches and a large thermos flask of tea. They each had a plastic cup with some tea resting by their knees between them, as they watched the ducks swim by and the fish resting in the shaded shallows.

He unwrapped from the cellophane another cheese-spread sandwich. After taking a bite, he picked up his cup and said softly, to reassure her, 'No, you're not. We all get nervous of change.'

'So you can see my point?' she asked as she stared aimlessly at the distant bank.

'Sure. Anyway, we don't know yet if you could get a transfer to that area, and I know we'd be very sad to see you go.'

'What?' She turned to him. 'You'd miss my great powers of detective and scientific reasoning?' And then she took a grated cheese-and-pickle triangle sandwich from her plastic box.

'No...' He let her take a big mouthful first before adding, 'You make a better cup of tea than Joe!'

They both laughed and for the first time that day she smiled.

'You know it's funny.'

'What is?'

'I don't know.' She glanced back over the river. 'It's like you're not just the guy I work with, but you're like a real best mate to me.'

'Thanks,' he replied, not sure how to answer.

'No, I mean it. I always know you're there in my corner ready to listen to my stupid problems.'

'Well, what are mates for.'

He sipped his tea as she picked a little at her sandwich and looked out over the river.

*

'But then that's you all over, isn't it?' The schoolgirl taunted her. 'Flirt with them, lead them on, pretend to be something special or some little victim to get their sympathy. But really you're just pathetic. You're a child. You're a selfish spoilt little brat and you care for no one or nothing but your own little sad life. You couldn't hold a relationship together for toffee. You can't let anyone get too close to you because if they do, they'll know just what a sad act you are! That's why you work as an environmentalist. Because trees don't ask you for favours. You're nothing more than a two-bit whore!'

'Stop it!' Ruth screamed as she turned away, a tear trickling from her eye. Quickly she wiped it way with a double sweep of her hand as the girl smiled.

'You okay?'

She turned to the platform entrance. Much to her relief, Paul was standing there, the sun behind him, casting him in a half-silhouette, creating a halo-like light around him as if his clothes were shining like armour.

'Yeah, I'm fine. Now I am.' She grinned.

'Schoolgirl trouble?' he asked.

'You could say that, yes!'

She looked around and noticed the schoolgirl was gone.

'Well, maybe this will cheer you up.' He crossed over to her.

'What is it?'

'Joe's found something which could be of some use to us.'

*

The monitor began to speed up. The signal was getting strong again.

20

Paul placed his empty paper cup next to the growing pile on the coffee table. The strip light above flickered twice, clunking away as if there was a moth trapped inside, before the light flicked back to life.

Joe was lying across three chairs, not asleep but a little drowsy, as John, arms and ankles crossed, stared hard at the top of the coffee table.

The sound of a trolley being wheeled passed the door and Paul looked over, as if he expected the door to open, but it didn't and he looked over to where Joe lay.

But just then the door did open. Joe began to sit up, rubbing the bridge of his nose, to bring the life back into his eyes. The doctor entered carrying a manila file.

'Gentlemen.'

All three turned to him and he spoke to them all as one.

'What's happening, Doctor?' John asked, sitting more upright and uncrossing his arms.

'I've just come to give you a progress report.'

'How serious is it?'

The doctor smiled uneasily as he opened the file and looked down at the sheet inside. 'She's out of immediate danger. We've stabilized her internal bleeding and set her fractures. Though she's still unconscious, she is responding well to treatment.'

'But there's something else, isn't there, Doctor?' Paul asked. The doctor grimaced uneasily.

'I'm afraid so. You see, you must understand that she took the full force of the impact.'

'And?' John asked nervously. He stood involuntarily as if he was ready to run down to the emergency ward and do whatever was needed to help her.

'And as a result, she has sustained a series of injures which, by their very nature, make it difficult for us to deal with all of them in one go.'

The strip light flickered again before its constant hum returned. The doctor continued. 'Also, we have arrested certain problems but while they were being cleared up, we discovered something else.'

He couldn't stand it any longer. John turned away, an icy shiver running down his spine. He crossed to the window and looked out over the car park to the town. The world was turning regardless. It felt as if they were living in another world and no one could help them. They were alone. He turned back.

'What?' Paul asked.

'She has suffered a brain haemorrhage....'

'NO!' Joe cried out in anguish.

'..... but at this stage it is not life-threatening though we will need to operate at once,' the doctor warned them.

'Will she pull through?' John asked quietly.

'If it wasn't for the fact we've already operated on her once already, and that her body is already in a poor state because of this and the accident, then I would say to you that the operation would be little more than a formality and that she would stand a good chance of a full recovery.'

'But because of her condition?' He was fearful of the answer but he had to know.

'I...' the doctor paused. He wanted to give them some hope but at the same time he didn't want to lie to them. 'I can only promise you that we will do all we can.'

'I see.' John understood.

'I'm sorry that I can't be any more helpful than that.'

The strip light began to flicker again and for a moment, it almost went out, fading to just a feeble glow inside the glass tube, but as John came over to the doctor, after more flickering the light came on.

'That's okay, we understand the situation. There's just one last thing?' John asked.

'Sure.' the doctor replied.

'Can we see her, before the operation?'

'Are you sure? Only I must warn you she is in a bad way.'

'Doesn't matter. Can we see her?'

'Wait here. I'll just arrange it for you.'

The doctor turned and left.

'Thank you.' John replied.

21

They had all arrived back at the station café. As before they were sitting around a table, near the platform window, each with a hot drink. Joe ate a big bag of crisps and grinned with pride as, in the middle of the table, with the ashtray and the condiments pushed to one side, there was a large, pristine, new timetable staring back at them.

'Where did you find this?' Paul asked as he took a sip of his drink.

'I managed to get into the ticket office from the platform entrance, just after the guard left to water the flowers,' Joe replied.

'I see.' Paul was impressed and a little disappointed for not thinking of doing that himself.

'So it's probably genuine,' John added.

'That's what I thought,' Joe continued. 'I mean, it wasn't just on the table. I had to find it.'

John looked down at the timetable, yet he still maintained a natural suspicion as nothing here could be taken at face value, but he couldn't help himself feeling a little excited that at last they had a chance to escape.

'So it could be the genuine article.' Ruth echoed his thoughts.

'Unless this is part of that schoolgirl's plans to wear us down,' Paul added, voicing the doubt they all felt inside.

'She doesn't have to be that devious. She's doing a pretty good job as it is already!' Ruth shuddered.

'True,' John agreed. 'But if they're so determined to keep you here so you can meet your so-called destiny, then we have to assume, even if this is genuine, that they'll know we have it!'

'And that they'll do all they can to prevent us from stopping the next train,' Paul added.

Joe nodded his agreement as Ruth sighed. 'And there I was, beginning to think we had a chance!'

'We do,' John assured her. 'After all, there's only two of them.'

'True.' Paul nodded and smiling to Ruth, he added, 'And four of us!'

'But if they know we've got a timetable, won't they do their best to defend the signal box?' she asked.

'Should imagine so!' John replied swinging the timetable round so he could examine it more closely.

'Crisp anyone?' Joe asked, offering the bag to the others.

'No thanks.' Ruth declined as the bag was almost pushed into her face.

'All we have to do then is give them something to watch,' Paul remarked.

'We've got a problem with this.' John spoke ominously.

'Oh, don't tell me it's out of date.' Ruth asked nervously.

'It can't be. I checked!' Joe replied.

'No,' John continued, 'it's not out of date. It's the trains.'

'What, I've already missed the last one?' she asked.

'No, not quite.' He frowned. 'There's two more today, one within the next hour, then one two hours after that. Then there isn't one until the day after next.'

'The day after I'm supposed to die?!'

'That's right,' he confirmed to her dismay.

'Two chances.' Paul took a deep breath. 'That's not many.'

'We only need one!' Joe reminded them positively, sensing they were already anticipating defeat.

'All we need then is a plan!' she exclaimed.

John smiled as he looked at her. She was beginning to show some of her fighting spirit. He admired that in her and suddenly he could feel an idea growing in his mind.

'What?' she asked.

'Trust me,' he replied.

She screamed.

It was as if a red-hot knitting needle had been poked into her eye. A searing pain, splitting apart her brain, as a high-pitched noise, like a claw scraping down a chalkboard reverberated around her skull, drowning out all other sound. The light was bright, swirling and burning, beginning to elongate the shapes around her, as they started then to spin.

The pain grew sharper.

The noise in her head grew louder.

The colours became much brighter.

She gripped her head as if she was trying to force away a vice clamped around her head. She fell forward, leaning on the table for support.

She screamed.

'You alright? John asked. He was shaken as she turned her ashen face from him. With Paul, he rushed to comfort her as she fell back in her chair.

22

She raised her arms to shield her face as the large tree loomed over her. The side of the car smashed into it and as her door began to buckle in towards her, the driver's window, the window beside it, the rear window and the front windscreen all turned white, then shattered, disintegrating into a showering hail of crystal, confetti-like shards of glass all about her, into her hair, into her clothes, into her hands, her arms.

It all went quiet and as she looked up, the whole world turned white.

*

'You okay now?' John asked moving her paper cup back beside her as she began to sit up.

'Uh-huh.' She nodded, her cheeks stained by her

tears.

She took a couple of deep breaths and began to relax. The pain was gone and she could feel the blood coursing through her body so that for a moment she felt a little giddy.

'You're looking a better colour now.'

'It's just a headache, that's all, like a migraine. It's probably the pressure of this place.' She smiled reassuringly at him, hoping he wouldn't worry.

'Well, don't let it get to you.' He touched her arm tenderly and for a moment she was sure she blushed. 'Because I think I have the plan to get us out of this place.' Joe and Paul pulled their chairs closer round him, as John continued. 'They'll be expecting us to take the signal box, right?'

'Uh-huh.' She agreed. It was the most logical place, because, as far as she knew, it was the only place she would be able to stop a train.

'But the tracks must lead somewhere, right?' John asked them all.

'You don't expect us to run to the nearest town down the tracks, do you?' asked Joe, who was more worried by the idea of running down the track than anything the guard and the schoolgirl might do.

'Shall I hit him or do you want to do it?' Paul asked.

'No, we need him.' John continued, 'Right, here's the plan....'

23

The monitor was beeping and the rocker arm of the artificial respirator rising and falling, when the door opened and the nurse led John, Joe and Paul into the ward.

Seeing her there, heavily bandaged, was too much for Joe. He shook, overwhelmed with fear, holding back his tears. He stood near to the back of the room as the nurse led John and Paul over to the bedside.

'I'm sorry but she's still unconscious.' The nurse apologised as John bent down beside Ruth and Paul kept himself a discreet pace away.

'That's okay. It's what we'd expected anyway.'

John pinched a tear away from his eye as he leant towards her head and whispered.

'Hang in there, pal. We're all here for you. You know us. We wouldn't miss this for the world!' He waited for her to respond, but there was only the rising and falling of the respirator arm. His voice almost lost in the noise of the machines around her bed, he whispered faintly, 'I love you.'

*

Joe entered the ticket hall, looking around as if it was his first time there. Empty as usual and he grinned, having expected nothing else. Then with a purposeful stride he walked over and tapped the glass of the ticket-office window.

He waited and was about to strike the glass again when the door at the back of the ticket office opened. Joe watched the guard and beamed a manically forced, pleasant smile as he waited for him to reach the window.

'How may I help you, sir?'

'I'd like a ticket to Canterbury, please.'

'I'm sorry. We don't sell tickets to Canterbury here,' the guard replied dryly.

'How about Ashford?' Joe grinned harder and it felt as if his cheeks were going to rip.

'Sorry, sir. I can't help you.'

'What about Faversham? I like Faversham.'

'We don't sell tickets, sir,' the guard replied forcefully.

'But this is the ticket window, right?' Joe asked.

'Yes sir, but we don't sell tickets.'

'Then I'd like a ticket to....'

'But we don't sell tickets!' the guard interrupted.

'Not even to Aylesham?'

'No, sir.'

*

The yard was empty, just as they expected, and keeping crouched low, John, Ruth and Paul, made their way along the front of the station. They reached the entrance door and crouched lower so they couldn't be seen through the station's windows. John peered in.

He could see Joe was still talking to the guard. He turned back to Paul and gave him a quick thumbs up. Paul stood as Ruth and John quickly scrambled over to the other side of the door and kept going, making their way past the phone box and to the fence that led back to the platform.

Paul stood by the door jamb, out of sight of the ticket hall as he watched the other two.

John carefully peered over the fence to check the platform was clear.

He turned back and signalled to Paul and, as Paul walked boldly into the station, John and Ruth quickly clambered over.

24

'How about a ticket to Herne Bay or Whitstable?' Joe asked, leaning on the counter to peer into the ticket office as Paul strode past behind him.

'For the last time, sir, we don't sell tickets. The trains don't stop here.' The guard sighed heavily.

Paul headed out onto the platform.

He walked over to the edge and looked both ways along the track.

'I wouldn't go any further if I was you, sir.' He heard a voice behind him and as he swung round, there, a few feet away from him, coming from the other end of the platform, was the guard.

He was shocked at first, then as the confusion clouded his mind, he stammered, 'How the...?'

'I wouldn't stand that close to the edge, sir, in case a train should pass, sir. You could end up getting injured.'

'Right.' Paul grinned, taking a half step over the white line. 'And how are you going to stop me?'

Behind the guard, he could just see Ruth and John as they slid down the fence and keeping up against the rails, they moved back closer to the main building, becoming hidden from his view.

Paul's attention switched back to the guard, who took out a small pistol from his jacket pocket and pointed it at him.

'I see.' Paul took a short step back from the platform's edge.

*

There was the distant sound of the engine's whistle and Ruth could see the steam from its funnel like a low, silver-grey cloud drifting over the green trees in the distance.

They still had plenty of time.

John glanced at his watch, 'It's on time.' He smiled. The timetable was genuine.

'At least that's one thing for this place!' Ruth sighed.

They looked to each other and after a moment he whispered, 'Good luck.'

*

The guard was getting frustrated now. He replied curtly as Joe stood there, smiling at him.

'We don't sell any tickets, sir.'

'That's okay. I don't really want to buy one anyway.' And before the guard could react, Joe ran for the platform.

'Wait!' the guard called, pressing his nose to the window.

Joe rushed onto the platform and skidded to a stop as the guard swung his aim from Paul to him.

*

Without another moment's hesitation, as the black shadow of the train began to appear on the horizon, John and Ruth ran and jumped off the edge of the platform. Then, as Ruth with all her might ran up the track away from the station, John sprinted over to the signal box.

*

He hopped over the rails and along the embankment towards the wooden steps that ran up the side of the brick section to the cream wooden hut with its green door at the top. Three of its walls overlooked the track, with their tall glass windows, separated by thin frames, giving the signal operator a full view of the entire track and station.

Inside he knew, not just would he be able to see everywhere around the station, but there he could control the levers to stop the train.

John ran over the last few loose chippings and reached the foot of the stairs. As he took hold of the rail and climbed the first two steps, a voice behind him said, 'I wouldn't if I was you, sir.'

He turned to see the guard standing just a few feet away, his gun pointing directly at him.

'Come down, sir. It's not worth it, is it, sir?'

John walked back down to the ground with his hands slightly raised as the guard indicated with his gun that he wanted him to head back to the platform.

*

Ruth was nearly out of breath. It was a hard run as the sleepers between the tracks were too far apart for her stride and she had to run against the loose chippings as she closed on the signal.

It stood on a large post, a white arm, with a black

chevron on it. At the post end was a black metal figure of eight with a red lens in the top eye and a green in the lower. The signal itself was pointing down to the ground, positioning the green lens over the white light that shone through it.

As she reached it, she looked behind her but there was no one chasing her. She looked along the track and could still see the smoke from the train coming down the line, but still a little way from the station.

She paused to look about her. She was alone. Then as she stepped up to the post looking for a lever or a way to change it manually, she noticed there was a metal ladder on the embankment side that reached up to the signal. She began to climb. The steps were close together and she had to hold the rungs ahead of her as there was no rail, no finger-holds to use along the sides. She had taken a few steps when she heard a rustling from the bushes below.

She looked back and there the guard stood, his pistol pointing up at her. He smiled.

'Come down, Miss. You can't change the signal from up there.'

'What you going to do shoot me?' She clung on to the rung and glanced back up at the signal. Fourteen rungs, that's how many she had left to climb.

'If I have to, Miss?'

'If you kill me now, what would that do for all your destiny and all that?' She taunted him, turning back to him.

'I have six rounds in my gun. I could hit you in each knee and each elbow and still have two rounds to fulfil your destiny tomorrow,' he replied dryly. 'Look at it this way, Miss. You can either live out your destiny in comfort or as a cripple? The choice is yours.'

'I suppose that's a choice!'

'So are you coming down, Miss?' He flexed his grip upon the pistol and after a moment's hesitation, she climbed down.

The guard took a few paces back, his eyes, watching

her like a hawk as she reached the ground. She turned back to him.

'Now what?' she asked.

'To the bank.' He waved her to the bank with the point of his gun and as she joined him, there was a shrill banshee-like scream and all around her the air was filled with the sound of rolling thunder and a thick, acrid smoke engulfed them both as the train rumbled by.

25

A light flashed.

Then it went dark.

A light flashed again, then dark.

There were squares of light and dark and she had a sense she was moving. Feet first. As if she was falling, but it didn't seem like she was falling as she felt she was lying on her back.

The light came and went, bright and dark. Then she felt herself drifting to her right. Her feet were turning and she followed.

As she moved, she could hear the constant roll of wheels and the bumping and clacking as they ran over a constant pattern of ribs on the ground.

Muffled noises, like talking but in a language she couldn't understand.

Suddenly she saw a face, upside down with a

moustache, smiling as he leaned over her. He spoke, but she couldn't hear his words. Suddenly there was a jolt and she felt her body shudder. She heard some double doors swing shut.

Darkness.

She closed her eyes. She was still falling. All the sounds echoed. It was like she was listening to it in water.

She was no longer moving.

Suddenly she was levitating in the darkness.

She opened her eyes.

Bright lights, circles of them, harsh and burning. She wanted to turn away, but she couldn't. People wearing face masks and soft cloth hats, that matched their long gowns, looked down at her, only their eyes visible. Babbling sounds bounced around her. She was confused but couldn't move before one of them clamped a harsh-smelling, black rubber mask over her nose and mouth.

She wanted to scream, but she couldn't.

As she tried to breathe, she was feeling weaker, feeling confused, drifting out of her body. She was feeling light and sleepy. Her eyelids were heavy. The light began to fall away as if it was receding into the distance, at the end of a long tube and then everything was gone.

She couldn't feel and hear anything any more.

*

The strip light flickered and began to hum.

They were back sitting in the hospital waiting room. Joe and Paul sat facing each other across the coffee tables, peering into the space between them. John remained standing and nervously crossed to lean against the wall near the door.

He felt so impotent.

'Won't make it happen any quicker,' Paul commented.

'I know,' John sighed.

'We've just got to trust them to do their best for her.

That's all.'

'Sure.'

'I hope she pulls through.' Joe added. 'I mean. She is a great mate to work with.'

'Know what you mean.' Paul replied. 'I think we would all miss her if she....'

'Stop it, will you?' John snapped. 'Stop it.' He calmed down. 'Stop talking about her as though she's going to die! She's not. Okay! Not if I have anything to do with it, she's not!'

'Problem is, mate, none of us have anything to do with it, do we?' Paul replied.

John looked away, as a tear welled up in his eye.

*

She turned her steering wheel. Her car lurched and skidded. The oncoming car's brakes squealed as it shuddered to an emergency stop. Her car just missed it and slewed sideways, skidding off the road between the chevron signs and towards a large oak tree.

She screamed as she held her arm up to her face.

The car smashed into the side of a large tree and as it shuddered against it, her door began to buckle in. The driver's door window, the window beside it, the rear window and the front windscreen, all turned white as they shattered, then disintegrated, showering the entire inner space of the car with droplets of glass.

*

As the surgeon and his staff worked on Ruth, her monitor beeped slowly, but steadily and her breathing remained constant as the anaesthetist kept a watchful eye over her.

26

The four of them were sat around a table, each with a hot drink as Joe ate another bag of crisps. The woman behind the counter was washing a cup as she slyly watched them. Dejected and hunched over the table, they knew they were being watched and, as the sound of her coffee maker warming the water echoed around, they talked in hushed voices so that she couldn't make out a word they were saying.

Paul shook his head as he played with the edge of the ashtray.

'I can't believe it!'

'I know.' John shook his head, finding the whole situation hard to understand. 'At first I thought it was more than one but after the train went by, I turned back and he was gone.'

'He was gone. Ours was reduced by half!' Joe ate

another crisp as Ruth turned to them all and looked at them each in turn.

'The point is,' She asked. 'how can one man be in four places at once?!'

'Nothing about this place makes sense, except for one thing.' John replied.

'What's that?'

'Putting what we believe about the world to one side for the moment, let us accept that there is a strange force about this place, right?'

'Go on?' Paul left the ashtray alone and listened closely.

'Well,' John began, 'for all their power, there is still one thing they can't control.'

'The trains?' Ruth asked. He smiled with a little nod.

'Exactly!' He leant a little closer into the group. 'It doesn't stop because they control the signals but they can't control it, itself. The fact they've spent so much time and energy defending those signals proves that. So, all the time there are trains running, we have a chance of getting out of this place!'

Joe took out the timetable and spread it between them, twisting it round for John to read.

'But you're forgetting one thing,' Ruth declared. 'I mean, I've probably had more experience of it than the rest of you, but when the guard stopped me up at the signal box, it occurred to me that they have the power to read our minds as well as be in more than one place at any one time. I mean, when you think about it, that's how that bloody schoolgirl knows so much about my past, my feelings and so forth?'

'True!' John replied.

'And it doesn't matter what we do,' added Paul as he continued, 'they'll always know what we're trying.'

'I know.'

'Well.' Joe was still looking at the timetable and had his finger under the train time. 'There's one more train in an hours' time. After that, there isn't one for another day.'

'And by then I'll be dead!' Ruth replied with a sarcastic laugh.

'At least we know the train's coming,' Joe replied helpfully.

'Well, unless they've made the book up between them, we know it's coming,' Paul added.

'I think it's the real thing,' John added reassuringly. 'The first train arrived to time and if that thing wasn't genuine, then why have they got every eye on us? George Orwell couldn't have imagined this level of surveillance!'

'I think you're right,' Ruth agreed. 'I can't see why they would want to pretend another train would be due, when they can always prevent us from stopping it. It's that girl's way of torturing me further. She's a right sadist! The knowledge that, yes, I have one more chance to escape my so-called destiny before then having a whole day to sit and wait around here in this hellhole for her to kill me is the most soul-destroying torment anyone could have ever devised!'

'So we have to stop this train at all costs?' Joe asked.

'Exactly.' John replied.

'But how?'

'Just think for a minute,' John continued. 'We know that they can read our minds! We also know that they know we know.'

'Here we go. Confuse us!' Paul grinned.

'So let's put the fact that they know we know that they know we know to our advantage,' John replied.

'How?' Ruth asked. He turned to her.

'By doing what we did before, but .... ' He began to grin broadly.

'But what?' She asked, bemused.

27

John came back into the room to sit by Paul. The strip light flickered and he thought he heard a trolley pass the waiting room, but no one came through the door.

Paul and Joe were still staring into the space above the city of paper cups on the coffee table and, as John sat on the hard, moulded plastic of the chair, he became restless, as if he couldn't stand the wait any longer.

He wasn't alone. The other two felt the same. John and Paul looked up as Joe suddenly stood.

'Anyone want anything to eat?' he asked. They shook their heads. He fumbled under his coat for some change as he left.

*

Ruth looked up, over to the signal box. She was

sitting alone on the bench at the far end of the platform. She watched the signal box, counting the number of steps, watching the windows to see if there was any movement inside and calculating the distance from the platform, over the two sets of tracks and the run along the embankment to the steps.

'Penny for them?' She turned round and there, like her shadow, stood the schoolgirl looking down at her.

'Oh, it's you.'

'Abandoned, are we?'

'No.' Ruth turned away and looked along the line. 'Just wanted some time on my own.'

'What?' The girl stifled an ironic laugh. 'To reflect on your destiny?'

'Get real!'

'So you still believe that you can leave here?'

'And why shouldn't I?' Ruth demanded to know. 'I am a valuable scientist. I must do all I can in order to continue my work for society.'

'How cute and oh how so very presumptuous of you.' The schoolgirl smirked. 'To have such blind faith in one's own abilities when in reality one would be hardly missed.'

'That's not true!' she snapped back.

'Isn't it? Or don't you remember that poisoning at Barham?'

28

Two phials were swirling around in the arms of the centrifuge. She watched the hands of the large beige clock with the two silver arms jutting out, one either side, and when the red second hand hit the hour mark again, she pressed the stop button on the centrifuge. As the rotating arms began to slow, she hit the left-hand lever on the clock. It stopped and she hit the right-hand lever to set all its hands back to twelve.

The lab door opened and, as she looked round, John entered carrying a small, thick, weaved canvas bag. As he placed it down on a nearby table, she slipped the cover off the top of the centrifuge and took the first of the two phials out.

'Ruth? Are those the samples from Barham?'

'Yes, I'm about to do the test on them now.'

He sat at the desk and began to unfasten the strap to

his bag.

'If we can trace the type of acid it is, then we can begin to eliminate the manufacturing companies in that area.'

'What do you think it's most likely to be?' she asked as she put some of the sample into a beaker. Then, after putting the phial in a rack next to it, she took the top off a dark-brown bottle of PH universal indicator.

'Paul thinks it's likely to be leakage from the cesspit, but if the levels are under 5.5 then it could be the nearby rubbish incinerator, burning materials before the furnace is hot enough.'

Using a pipette, she added some of the PH indicator to the sample in the beaker and watched as it turned bright blue.

'John?'

He turned to her as she held up the beaker for him to see.

'Alkaline? But that's impossible.'

'But.... I've done the test correctly,' she replied, confused and baffled.

'But that would indicate heavy metals, but the plants are scorched. And anyway, there's no heavy-metal type of industry in that area for miles!'

'But... I... I don't know what.'

'Bring the samples over here,' he beckoned her over to him, 'and I'll check it.'

She picked up her file and notes and brought them over to his desk.

*

'Turned out you'd labelled the specimens wrong,' the schoolgirl sneered, 'and had been testing an old industrial site in South-East London.'

'But my testing was right, even though I got it wrong. We all make mistakes from time to time. To err is human!'

102

'Some more than most,' the schoolgirl taunted her. 'But I get it right as well.'

29

A dappled light filtered through the thick tree canopy, which was swaying gently as the wind rustled through the thin branches. Yet all around her it was still.

She could hear birds in the distance, but none were nearby. Only the sound of the fast-moving water lapping over stones and through the reeds at the river's edge roared like a distant rock concert around her.

A little way behind her, by a fallen tree, where there was a gap in the canopy, John was labelling up some sample jars and recording their details into his notebook. Out in the river, with his long, green waders on, stood Joe, the water just over halfway up his leg as he twisted a handheld auger into the riverbed.

'That's the sheep dip, the bank, the field and the riverbed once Joe stops faffing about and gets us the sample,' John called.

'It's not easy, you know,' Joe called back, 'it's up to my knees!'

Ruth grinned, as John replied.

'If you wanted an easy job with no responsibilities, you should have gone into politics!'

'On days like this I wish I had!'

She watched as he pulled the auger out and started to wade over to her. From her bag she took out a specimen jar and unscrewed the lid. When he reached her, he held the auger over the jar and pushed the soil sample in with his fingers.

'I can't help thinking we're missing something.' She screwed the lid back on as she then made her way over to John.

'Something's killing the river weed, and if we don't find it soon, all the fish will die.'

'But Paul took samples of all these areas last time,' she reminded him, as something inside told her to expect the result to be the same.

'Maybe whatever it is was flushed out of the river last time?'

'Possibly, but if that's so, then the cause has to be industrial, right?'

'Which is why we've got a sample of the sheep dip,' he reminded her.

'But unless he's using a new brand, we've already eliminated that idea!'

'Look around you.' He stood and she looked with him across to the other side of the river. 'We've a farm, a small town over the hill and a large wood. There's no heavy industry in this area.'

'What about a mine?' She asked.

'Nearest one was Hersden which is forty miles away. And anyway, that's downstream. The chances of the materials seeping out somewhere around here are even more remote than us finding an industrial site!'

'What about an old factory?' she continued. 'You

know, like a paper mill or a landfill site which was once a quarry?'

'There's nowhere around here which would suggest a mill of any kind. The river's too narrow.'

Joe threw his auger to the bank and, holding the tufts of grass, with a little struggle hauled himself up out of the river.

'But there could be something?' she asked, determined they should look elsewhere.

'Where?' John pointed around as if he needed a clue where to start.

'I think we should look upstream,' she replied. 'I mean the contamination has to come from upstream.'

'Why?' Joe asked picking up the auger and slipping the wooden handle out of the eye-hole as he joined them.

'Because the river begins to slow here,' she replied. 'It's fastest upstream, so if there is a leaking pipe or something contaminating the river and the particles which are killing the plant life are being flushed away, here's where they're pooling. But they aren't killing anything after the weir.'

'Where the river widens and runs faster.'

'Then here isn't the primary location. This point is between the source and the weir, but the damage here, though bad, isn't being caused by anything too toxic, or it would be killing the fish and reeds and other wildlife way, way past the weir too. So, the source is probably not too far from this point here as this is where the worst of the damage is taking place!'

'Would make sense,' Joe agreed.

She turned back to John.

'Would also explain why Paul found nothing.'

'Suppose you have a point,' he conceded as he picked up the sample bag. 'Joe.' He held it out towards him. 'Take this back to the truck and dry yourself off. We're going to take a quick look upstream.'

'Right.' Joe took the bag.

With the samples and tools, Joe headed up the small, dirt track towards the five-bar gate where their truck stood, as Ruth and John, headed deeper into the wood.

*

They followed the river as it began to narrow and meander into the wood, and after a while they come across an old, rusting, chain-link fence stretching from the bank and through the trees barring their way.

In some places there were gaps in the fence and in other places some of the fixings had rotted away, leaving parts of the fence hanging limp between the metal posts.

'Funny place to put a fence,' Ruth remarked as John looked at his map.

'There's no indication of any private land on this map.'

'When was it printed?'

'Two years ago.'

'So whatever this is, it's been forgotten about,' Ruth replied as she felt the coarseness of the rust between her fingers and noticed how it stained them.

'Looks like it.' He shrugged, scratching the back of his head as Ruth followed the fence down to the river edge. He stood by the fence and peered into the dense mat of overgrown brambles and skinny trees.

'What can you see?' she called.

'Hard to say.' He strained his eyes as though they were binoculars, as if by doing so, he would be able to see more clearly what was in front of him. 'It's all so overgrown.' His eyes caught something. 'But there looks to be the remains of a building or works or something and maybe two troughs or something in the ground.'

'Maybe it's an old military testing site.'

'Not from World War Two.'

'How can you tell?'

'It would be on my map!'

There was a large tree, on the river's edge barring her way round. It was so big, with its roots protruding out of the side of the bank and into the water, she surmised that it had been used as part of the fence structure when the fence had originally gone up. She could see just at shoulder height, at right angles to the bank, there was a long, drooping branch and, using the trunk to support her, she reached out and grabbed it. She swung herself out so she was leaning over the water, her feet, almost on tiptoe, still standing on the edge of the bank.

She looked along the bank and began to smile as she could see a pipe a few feet above the water level sticking out of the ground. She turned to look back to where John was standing and in doing so, her hand on the tree trunk slipped and before she could steady herself, she lost her grip on the branch and she fell into the river.

Quickly he ran over to her.

'You alright?'

Ruth looked up at him. She was sitting up to her waist in the fast-flowing water. A cloud of mud billowed and drifted away.

'Yeah.' She winced slightly because the riverbed was stony. 'I'm fine.' She shifted herself in the water. 'Bruised my bum, but otherwise nothing damaged.'

John held onto the tree as he leant towards her, holding out his hand as she stood and he helped her back onto dry land.

She noticed him twitch slightly as he was desperately trying not to laugh.

She wiped the hair from out of her eyes. They stood there for a moment looking at each other, as somewhere overhead in the canopy a bird was singing.

'You alright?' he asked.

'Oh, yes, yes. I've er... found it.'

'Eh?'

'The source of the contamination. There's a pipe probably running back to the works there. Looks like it originally had a cover over it, but that's gone, probably damaged in a storm or something, and now if it rains, the pipe fills when the river swells.' She pointed up the stream.

'And you reckon that every time that happens, the flood washes the contaminants into the river?'

'Uh-huh.' She nodded.

'Great. We'll take a sample from the pipe right away.' She smiled as he looked her up and down adding. 'Come on, we'd better get you dry.'

30

'Had been an old TNT factory, set up during the First World War. Apparently, the businessmen of the time were encouraged to put some of their money into funding the war effort from 1915 onwards when it was clear we needed more shells, more quickly. No planning permission, just some land was all that was needed. All secret. Even the women who worked there couldn't say what they were doing, even though the processes involved used to turn their skin yellow. Factories like that sprang up all over the place. This one, though only small, had been set up on an old dairy by the river. After the war, they'd just abandoned it. But there was some TNT left there. TNT is acidic. It corrodes metal and poisons water organisms and might even be carcinogenic in fish! Over the decades, it had corroded the storage tanks and rain coming into the old huts had washed it into the river.

Without my persistence, we would never have found the source until it was too late.'

'Ooh, who's a Miss Know-It-All!' sneered the schoolgirl.

'No, not a know-it-all, but I do know how you use what I know.'

'What do you mean?'

A gentle breeze drifted across the platform as they both stared hard at each other, the sound of the clock breaking the silence.

'You like trains?' Ruth replied.

'I love trains. That's why I'm here. My father's a member of the local Steam Railway Appreciation Society.'

'Is that why you live in the signal box?'

'I don't know what you mean.' The schoolgirl twisted uneasily on her heels and Ruth realised she'd struck a nerve with the girl, found out her secret and suddenly, she felt empowered.

'Well, there's another train due soon, and someone has to change the points and the signals or else it will stop.'

'I don't understand what you're saying.' The schoolgirl was becoming disorientated, confused. Her overbearing self-confidence was quickly eroding from her as with a knowing grin Ruth asked, 'Where were you when we tried to stop the other train?'

'Really!' She was getting flustered. 'I don't have to answer your questions!'

'You see, I know where to go if I want to stop a train and you can't stop me.'

The schoolgirl suddenly became calm and confident again, her sudden panic over. She looked at Ruth, her head slightly tilted and grinned.

'Are you sure about that?'

'Eh?'

'You knew what you wanted with Simon. Couldn't make him change his mind, could you?'

Ruth was puzzled and began to feel a little concerned

as she asked, 'In what way?'

'Couldn't make him want you, could you?' The girl grinned. 'Because you're nothing more than a stick-on-legs and about as much fun to fuck as a balloon! Only a balloon has better conversational skills and foreplay than you'll ever have.'

'Shut it!' She screamed, near to tears.

'Struck a chord there?' The girl rocked back on her heels, a feeling of satisfaction welling up inside her. 'You hopeless excuse for womanhood. Couldn't keep a man if you chained him to the bed and pumped his brain with Novocaine. And you want to stop the train. You're a glutton for punishment, that's all I can say!'

Ruth began to cry.

31

The lounge was a long room with a door at one end that led into the kitchen and another halfway along the longest wall that led to the corridor and to the other rooms as well as the front door.

The lounge itself was divided by the furniture into two halves. Furthest from the kitchen facing the television unit were a sofa and an armchair around a low coffee table, with a top made of black, grey and white mosaic tiles, sitting on a rug with a swirling pattern of three shades of red. On the unit stood a large television, and on the shelf above the cupboard space, there was the VCR player, games console, with its own tape player, and behind the smoked-glass cupboard doors a number of VCR tape cassettes and game cartridges stood side on, like a row of books on a library shelf, staring back into the room.

Behind the sofa, there was a round, glass-top dining

table with four chairs, with, at its centre, a wicker bowl of fruit, apples, oranges and a couple of bananas. Between the two sets of windows sat a sideboard, on which were a number of photos of Ruth and Simon on their holidays in Spain as well as two single, clear-crystal, Victorian style candlesticks.

On the short wall by the kitchen hung a large black-and-white print of a starfish on a bed of pebbles and on the wall facing the sofa, there was another large print, of Edward Hopper's The Nighthawks.

They were both snuggled up together on the sofa, the remotes on the coffee table and Ruth's bare feet curled up under her. She held an almost empty wine glass in her hand, the half-empty bottle of Merlot on the coffee table next to Simon's empty glass.

'That film you want to see is on after this?' he asked, as he wondered why he was enduring a show he had little interest in with a cast of nonentities he cared even less about.

'Oh good.' She snuggled herself into him some more. 'I've been dying to see it.'

He shifted a little uneasily, but she thought nothing of it, as she knew the show they were watching was dull, but it was killing the time before what she wanted to watch would start.

'Ruth?' He sounded a little detached.

'What?'

'I suppose this is as good a time as any, only I've got something to tell you.'

'What's that?'

He freed himself from her and as she sat up, slipping her feet out to the rug, he leant forward and poured himself some wine, offering some to Ruth, before topping up her glass when she replied with a nod.

'I've got through to the interview, for the promotion.' He put the bottle down.

'Oh.' She didn't know what to say. She felt numb, but

she didn't understand why.

'Well, you could at least sound as though you're happy for me.'

She sat up a little. 'I am,' she insisted but she didn't even sound convinced to herself.

'Are you?'

'Really, I am. It's wonderful news for you.'

'For us surely?' he reminded her as he took a sip of his wine.

'Yes.... whatever?'

'They seemed very positive about my prospects. It looks as though I could get the job!' he added proudly.

'Oh.' She looked away. 'I see.'

'The area doesn't look too bad either. I think we could be very happy living there.'

Ruth felt a rush of fear suddenly well up inside her, making her shiver slightly. She turned to him. She knew she was about to hurt him and that upset her, but inside she also felt the immense turmoil, the feeling of loneliness, that she had no one to turn to, to voice her fears to, and a loathing that she was being forced to feel this way. Her dreams and desires were being questioned, as if she was being asked to sacrifice something which was pulling her. The wrench of it made her tremble and fell as confused as a junkie going cold turkey. Her wants and desires were being treated as if less important because they were hers. She wanted to scream at him, but instead she took a sip of wine and looking him sorrowfully in the eye, she replied.

'I, Simon, I can't get a transfer there.'

There was some canned laughter from the television and everything else went quiet. His happy face slid to one of repressed anger as the implications of what she was telling him slowly sank in.

'Look, hon! I know how much your job means to you but, look, I'm sure there will be others just like it nearby. Look, this is a golden opportunity for us. I've got to take it, haven't I?'

If he knew how much her job meant, he wouldn't have said it. It was there, in the open, the moment she feared. His career was important. In his mind, she thought, her career was like little more than a hobby, something to give up when there was something more important to do.

She could see it now. She'd be the little hausfrau, making sure his dinner was ready for when the brave little soldier was home from slaying all those industrial dragons. A cold shiver ran down her spine. She felt as if the walls were closing in, that she was suddenly a prisoner, a number, her name and her place in the world removed and for what?

She wanted to be free, to have a role, a purpose, a life of her own, her way and to hold dear that right to explore and find that purpose for herself. She didn't want to be forced into living someone else's dream. She accepted that maybe one day she might like the idea of taking on that role of homemaker, but in her own time, if it was for her, and he couldn't see it. Not yet. It was like she wasn't a complete person in his eyes. It was as if she was there only to support his life and make his life complete.

'Oh course you have,' she replied as she stood up and placed her glass down on the coffee table.

'Where you going?' he asked, somewhat confused.

'I thought I might have a bath.'

'But the film?'

'It's alright. I'm sure they'll repeat it again sometime.'

She didn't know why she felt like she did. Was she really being just selfish or was it a fear of commitment? Simon was right. She could easily have found another job, a woman with her qualifications. But she supposed it was a selfishness she had within her as she couldn't see herself giving up the job she had.

She left the room and closed the door gently behind her.

*

'However, until it was confirmed I had always assumed it wasn't going to happen. But he won his promotion and so had to move. The problem was I didn't want to.'

*

The night outside was dark, no stars, only the harsh glare of the nearby streetlamp spilling on the window frame.

They were eating dinner, facing across their dining table, eating in silence, only the scraping of their blades across their plates to accompany them.

He stopped for a moment and watched her as she piled some more food onto her fork.

'For crying out loud, say something?'

She paused and looked at him.

'About what?'

'Look.' He sighed heavily. 'We can't keep on living like this and not talking to each other!'

'Can't we?'

'No, of course not! Look Ruth, what's wrong? We're supposed to be happy. I've won my promotion, the lot. Why aren't you happy?'

'Because....' was all she could offer. He found her so infuriating.

'It's your bloody job, isn't it?'

'What do you mean, my bloody job?' she snapped back.

'Well it is, isn't it?'

'What if it is?' she replied angrily.

'Come on, Ruth. It's only a job.'

She was seething now. 'What do you mean it's only a job?'

'What I mean is you could give it up tomorrow. My promotion will be more than enough to cover the loss of your wages.'

'Oh, great.' She continued to eat, ignoring him as she angrily thrust some food into her mouth.

'I mean, it's not as though you can have a real career anyway!'

She slammed her fork down. 'And what's that supposed to mean?'

'Well, you being a woman!'

'You're saying because I'm a woman my career doesn't count for much?'

'Of course not!' He tried to backtrack but already he knew he'd gone too far.

'Then what are you saying?' she demanded to know.

'Well, you know, one day we might start a family. Then you'd have to give it up, wouldn't you? I mean, whether you have it at thirty or forty, you're going to have to give up your job. If you wait too long you'd be so old that you'd probably be dead before it starts secondary school!'

'We don't know that! I might be able to balance both!'

'Unlikely though, isn't it?' He watched her as she froze, fixing her stare on him.

'Don't know,' she began. 'I mean, you could lose your job and become a househusband.'

'As if!' He rolled his eyes which made her feel even angrier.

'I just think it's very selfish of you to assume that I will give up my life and follow you to the God-knows-where ends of the country for you without it mattering one little bit about what I want in all of this!'

'So you don't want to go?' he asked.

'No.' It was said at last.

'If you don't come....' he paused as he contemplated his next move carefully. '.... then it's over between us. There can be no going back.' She didn't respond and for what seemed like a lifetime they sat there, looking at each other.

'So?' he asked. 'You still staying?'

She picked up her fork and continued eating her dinner.

*

'Maybe the cracks had been there for some time. Maybe it was just me. But after that night. It was obvious to us both that it was over and shortly after that he was gone, out of my life forever.'

32

She looked up to the platform clock, it read 11:58.
'And you've been a sad act ever since.'
Ruth looked away as the schoolgirl began to smile to
herself, sensing she was getting under Ruth's skin.
'Ruth?' She looked round and there was John
standing behind her. 'It's time to head back to the café.'
She stood and looked around her, but the schoolgirl
had vanished.
'You alright?' he asked.
'Of course. Just that girl again.' She sighed.

*

The strip light flickered, the door opened and as Joe,
Paul and John turned from their thoughts to the door, the
doctor entered.

'Well, Doctor?' Paul asked.

'We've done all we can for her,' he replied. 'It's up to whether she has the will to live or not now.'

*

She looked up at the station-café clock.

It was still 11:58.

Around the table, the four of them were nursing their drinks as John looked at the others in turn.

'Okay. It's time. Let's do it.'

He sat back as Joe stood. The rest sipped their drinks. Joe steadily and calmly made his way out of the café, under the ever-watchful gaze of the woman behind the counter.

John counted to forty in his head and then pushed his chair back noisily, making the woman watch him as he too left the café.

'Smile.' Paul encouraged Ruth. She smiled meekly but inside she was too nervous. Then she stood and left as Paul sat quietly and finished his drink.

*

In the signal box, the schoolgirl was sitting on a low cupboard at the far end of the room, watching, the door. Next to her on the wall there was a phone, and on the cupboard there was a kettle, two brown enamel mugs and a standard chess set.

The rest of the room was a long space, with a dozen levers, some coloured green, some red, but they all had a long, brass handle with a matching, long, brass, braking lever that had to be pulled in first before the signal lever could be pulled back or pushed forward along a slot that was a yard long in the floor. The levers ran the full length of the long wall of windows and on the windowsill, below them, one for each lever, there was a gauge and above the central window there was a bell that would ring every time one of the gauges flickered.

In the ceiling there was large bulb in a small, flat, triangular shade which illuminated a dull, yellow light and above the door there was a large, round clock with Roman numerals showing the time to be 11:58.

> *The tunnel of darkness,*
> *Beckons in times weighted,*
> *Cold heart so fair,*
> *Relax to the never ending.*
> *Let all hope and love subside,*
> *As with the diamond point of my knife,*
> *I will cut free*
> *The coil that retains you here,*
> *Slipping down Morpheus river,*
> *The quiet lamb no longer bleats,*
> *As her blood mingles with her memory.*
> *This is how it must be.*
> *So,*
> *Let the darkness flow,*
> *Down the river of life's reasoning.*
> *Let emotion go,*
> *As you enter into death's dawning.*
> *Be released and free,*
> *You now belong to me!*

She moved a white pawn on the chess set one space.

33

Joe walked boldly into the ticket hall and looked around. It was empty and so he strode over to the ticket office and peered inside.

No one was there. Just like before, he grinned. He knocked twice on the glass, waited, then knocked again and as he did so, the guard stepped out from the back room and crossed over to him.

'How may I help you, sir?' he asked.

'I'd like a ticket to Canterbury, please.' Joe smiled confidently.

'I'm sorry. We don't sell tickets to Canterbury here.'

'How about Ashford?'

'Sorry, sir,' the guard insisted. 'I can't help you.'

'What about Faversham? I like Faversham.'

'We don't sell tickets, sir,' the guard replied firmly yet courteously.

'But this is the ticket window, right?' Joe asked.
'Yes, sir, but we don't sell tickets.'
'Then I'd like a ticket to....'
'But we don't sell tickets.'
'Not even to Aylesham?' Joe asked.
'No, sir.'

*

There was no one about. The front of the station was clear and so, keeping themselves low below the windows, John, Ruth and Paul, made their way along the front of the building, and as they reached the entrance door and crouching lower so they couldn't be seen from within the station. They paused there a moment, making sure they were still unobserved before John peered in side.

He could see Joe was still talking to the guard. He turned back to Paul and gave him a quick thumbs up. Paul stood as Ruth and John quickly scrambled over to the other side of the door and continued, making their way past the phone box and to the fence that divided the yard from the platform.

Paul stood by the door jamb, out of sight of the ticket hall watching the other two get into position.

John carefully peered over the fence. The platform was clear.

He turned back and signalled to Paul, and as Paul walked boldly into the ticket hall, John and Ruth quickly clambered over the fence.

*

'How about a ticket to Herne Bay or Whitstable?' Joe asked. The guard sighed, trying to mask his irritation.

'For the last time, sir, we don't sell tickets. The trains don't stop here.'

Paul walked through to the platform, not pausing to

see what Joe was up to, and walked over to the edge of the platform before looking both ways along the track.

34

'I wouldn't go any further if I was you, sir.'

He turned slowly and, trying not to grin, Paul turned to see the guard standing next to him.

'You again?'

'I wouldn't stand that close to the edge, sir....,' he pointed to the white line at the edge of the platform, 'in case a train should pass, sir. You could end up getting injured.'

Behind the guard, he could just see Ruth and John as they slid down the other side of the fence and keeping up against it, they moved back closer to the main building, becoming hidden from his view.

He turned back to the guard, who pulled out a small pistol from his jacket pocket and pointed it at Paul.

'I see.'

*

In the distance there was the whistle of an engine and they could see the steam from its funnel like a low, silver-grey cloud billowing over the green trees in the distance.

Quickly John and Ruth edged closer to the track as the train came into view over the horizon. John glanced at his watch. 'It's on time.'

'As before.' Twice in a row she thought to herself. If only the normal rail service was a reliable. 'Good. I hate long waits.'

They turned to each other and he gave her a quick encouraging wink. 'Good luck' and he patted her gently upon the shoulder.

*

The schoolgirl began to swing her legs as she watched the door. She turned to the chess set and after a moment's deliberation, she moved the black knight out ahead of the pawns.

*

'We don't sell any tickets, sir.' The guard sighed as Joe tapped twice on the shelf under the ticket window.

'That's okay. I don't really want to buy one anyway.' Then suddenly he turned and ran for the platform.

'Wait!' the guard called.

*

Joe ran onto the platform, but slid to a stop as the guard swung his aim from Paul to him.

*

As the black shadow of the train began to come into view on the horizon, John and Ruth ran and jumped off the edge of the platform. Together, they hopped over the rails of the two sets of track, leaping across the sleepers and onto the loose gravel chippings on the far side and ran as fast as they could along the side of the tracks towards the signal box.

*

The schoolgirl swung her legs as she watched the door and smiled. She could sense Ruth was on her way.

*

She slipped a couple of times, but she was determined to reach the signal box. It was hard running on the loose stones, but she could see the wooden steps and she could see that the signal box's door was slightly ajar.

With all her might, she forced herself and soon she reached the steps. She was ahead of John and she grabbed the handrail. As she took the first three steps, a voice behind them called.

'I wouldn't if I was either of you.'

They turned to see the guard pointing his gun at them.

'Come down.' He waved with his gun to them to come over to him. 'It's not worth it, is it?'

John grinned, then turned, his hands slightly raised as he came slowly towards the guard, who indicated with his gun for them to head back to the platform. Suddenly John grabbed at the guard's arm, holding the gun away from him as they begin to grapple with each other.

'Go for it, Ruth!' he shouted as turned and ran up the steps without looking back.

She reached out for the door handle. A gunshot rang out and as she took hold of the door handle, a searing pain shot through her brain, causing her to rock on her heels and almost lose her balance. She reached out to steady herself. She felt as if she was about to fall and the world began to whirl around her into a twisting, merging, swirl of white light.

35

Her car was racing very quickly down the narrow lane, the green banking and the trees above blurring past as she looked down to her radio and twisted the knob, filling the interior with music.

It wasn't what she wanted so she leant over to the other knob and began to move it slightly. The white line between the two sets of numbers began to move along the slider as the sound drifted into a wash of static before another more mellow song, more suitable for driving, began to beat out from the speaker.

At the end of the road a sharp bend, with two set of chevrons pointing to the bend, began to close on the little car as it hurtled towards them.

She looked up and to her shock, she realised that she was approaching the bend.

'What?!....' she cried as her foot slammed onto the

brake.

Her car began to dance on its wheels and then skid from side to side as it tried desperately to stop, smoke rising from under the squealing tyres. There was a bang as the left front tyre burst. The car sank to its left and suddenly it began to slide across to the other side of the road.

The steering wheel became light and she fought to keep the car in a straight line.

The car began to take the bend on the wrong side of the road as headlights from another car met the lights of hers. The other car's headlights streamed into her cab, blinding her. She quickly pulled the wheel to her left with all her might, hoping to steer out of the other car's way.

Her car sliced past the oncoming car. Its brakes screeching, it came to an emergency stop and the two cars missed each other by just a few feet. But the little Mini bounced and swung into a 180 degree turn, before it skidded off the road, just missing the chevrons as it careered off sideways towards a large oak tree.

She could see the tree coming towards her. She screamed and held her arms up to shield her face as the car smashed into the side of the large tree. The Mini shuddered against it, her door began to buckle in, as the driver's door window, the window beside it, the rear window and the front windscreen, went white, shattering, then disintegrating, showering the entire interior with glass.

Everything suddenly stopped moving and she slammed into the side of the door and was thrown back across her seat to slump down across the space between the two front seats.

She opened her eyes.

Everything was black but for a couple of lights on her dashboard. There was a ticking sound. A green light flashed on and off with the ticking and she could smell petrol.

Suddenly a brilliant white light spread across the

bonnet of her car. She could see it illuminate the shattered fragments in the crumpled frame where her windscreen had been and, as she tried to look up, into the light appeared two silhouettes. One was a young girl, no older than eleven going by her shape and height, dressed in a long skirt and with a hat resting on the back of her head, creating a black halo, making it seem larger than normal. Next to her, was the silhouette of a man wearing a Breton-like hat.

The man and the girl made their way down to her car, but they couldn't see Ruth, still slumped over to the passenger seat.

'Hello? Are you alright?' the man called.

She tried to call out, but couldn't. She couldn't feel her jaw, her arms, her body. It was as if she had become totally numb.

'Are you okay?' the girl called.

'Stay up here. I'm going to take a look' she heard him say.

'Okay, Daddy.'

She turned her eyes to the light as the man's silhouette came closer. It crossed past the front of her car and she heard her car door open. She tried to look round, but couldn't move. She couldn't see him.

'Oh my God.' His breath was robbed from him by the shock of what he was looking at.

She heard him turn away and begin to scramble up the bank to the girl.

'How is she, Daddy?'

'I must phone for an ambulance, I..., she's alive.' He didn't sound so sure. 'You better... No wait.'

'What should I do, Daddy?'

He reached into his coat pocket and pulled out a pocket torch which he turned on.

For a moment, she saw their faces, as the torchlight lit them up. She could see them just over the edge of the windscreen frame, a schoolgirl, from a private school she guessed, with short, strawberry ginger hair and a nondescript man with a hat.

'Talk to her. Whatever you do, don't let her slip away. She must stay conscious. Talk to her about anything, but don't let her go!!'

The man's silhouette started to work its way back up the slope.

'Hello, you down there,' the timid voice of the girl called. 'I've got to talk to you, or else you'll slip away and we don't want you to do that. Do you like trains? I said do you like trains? I love trains.'

Ruth wanted to laugh. With that hat, he looked like an old-fashioned railway station guard.

'That's why I'm here. My father's a member of the local Steam Railway Appreciation Society. I say, do you play chess?'.

36

Still holding her head, Ruth flung the door open and entered the signal box. She looked up, straight into the eyes of the schoolgirl.

*

In the stillness of the emergency ward, the monitors connected to Ruth's motionless body, continued to beat at a steady rate.

*

The door rattled against its frame, and slowly closed behind her. Her head wasn't hurting anymore. The pain was little more than a dull memory as she crossed the room to the schoolgirl.

'I say, do you play chess?' The girl pointed to the set beside her. The game was well underway. Several pieces of both colours had been removed, but all the key pieces were still present.

'Sometimes.'

'So do I.' The schoolgirl smiled, wide-eyed and excited as if she was contemplating some new mischief.

'Simple game, isn't it?'

'If you say so.' Ruth shrugged.

'Doesn't take much skill or intelligence, chess and games like it. I mean, you know, a game that relies upon the accident of many variables. If you could concentrate on them all the time, then no one could ever win or lose! Not like draughts, where there are no variables, only directions. A much more complicated game, don't you think?'

'I've never given it much thought!'

'I suppose you wouldn't.' The schoolgirl sneered, then moved another white piece as Ruth turned her attention to all the levers.

'There's a lot of them, isn't there?'

'What do they all do?' Ruth asked.

'Some stop the train, some keep it going, some move the points to keep it going and one and one only will make it stop at our station.'

She glanced back to the girl. 'Which one?'

'Wouldn't you like to know?'

She quickly took hold of one of the levers and was just about to pull it when she stopped and looked back to the schoolgirl, who was grinning at her like a Cheshire cat.

'Why did you stop?'

'You'd like me to pull that one, wouldn't you?' Ruth snapped back.

'Life is like a game of chess,' the girl continued, 'so simple anyone can play it and so boringly tediously that for most of us, we haven't the courage to take on the variables, so we end our lives achieving little more than a stalemate.

But if you challenge the variables, then you might, only might though, end up scoring a checkmate.'

'Or being in checkmate myself!'

'That's the toss-up between good and evil and the payback for the past mistakes lying in your wake.'

'By evil,' asked Ruth, 'you mean what is considered wrong morally by society?'

'In part,' the schoolgirl agreed.

'And what's the other part?' Ruth asked.

'The evil we do to ourselves,' the girl replied. 'If we treat others differently to how we would have them treat us, whether by having an affair and denying them the right to do so too, or to say that to have an affair is wrong when we do it ourselves, to the simplest of sins, where we expect others to treat us with respect and in doing so treat them as though they are not worthy of it. Then we can find ourselves in check.'

'But that can happen to us and does happen to all of us at some time.' Ruth reasoned.

'But is your motive pure?' asked the schoolgirl as she continued. 'Granted we all make mistakes! To err is to be human and to forgive is to be a saint. Those we cannot be held accountable for! But if the pain you're causing deliberately to satisfy yourself and yourself alone, regardless of motive or desire, that's evil. If it's a by-product of something which is done on the side of right, then there is no comeback at all!'

*

In the stillness of the emergency ward, the monitors connected to Ruth's motionless body, began to slow in pace.

*

'Pull a lever,' the girl goaded her, 'any lever and

discover your destiny!'

Ruth grabbed another lever then, looking at the schoolgirl, she cried, 'I've always done what I've believed to be right. I've nothing to fear.'

'Then why don't you want to die?'

'Because I love life!'

'But you don't have a love in your life!' She taunted Ruth.

'I ....'

'Simon left you. A man you said you wanted to spend the rest of your life with!'

'But I have my career.'

'And what's that?' The schoolgirl asked. 'No one ever thanks you for it, and when you reach sixty or so, you'll be washed up and abandoned by a state that's bled you in order to feed its own corrupt ego! Left alone without ever tasting love. Life is so insignificant. Can't you see that? The many multi-billions of stars and, if you accept it, one God of creation, who created this life and the life on all those other planets and for what? It certainly wasn't to slave away until you're sixty or so and then spend the next fifteen to twenty years alone and bored. If you can't live with life, then you might as well make a space and let someone who can live with it use it instead!'

'That's not fair!' Ruth was near to tears.

'Isn't it?' the girl asked. 'Why couldn't you keep Simon?'

'We drifted apart. It happens.'

The schoolgirl smiled, swinging her feet against the cupboard, her heels echoing as they kicked the door.

'Or were you just selfish?' she asked. 'It was alright all the time he'd spend money on you, help you meet people but the moment you had to do something for him, it was too much of an effort for you.'

'It wasn't like that. I loved him at the time.'

'Or what he could bring you!'

'No!' Ruth shouted.

*

The monitors slowed.

37

'No.' Ruth repeated as she continued. 'I did love him at the time. But I changed.' She looked at the schoolgirl. 'He changed.'

'Love doesn't change.' She moved the black queen.

'No...? But it does.... It changes like when you pass through a waterfall. It changes because what is on the other side of the waterfall is not the same as what is on the original side and, unless you both want what's on the other side, one of you remains cut off by the water and the more waterfalls you pass through on your own, the more water there is between you.'

'But you're not worth anything?' The schoolgirl taunted her again, moving a white knight. 'Worth nothing to anyone but yourself! What sort of flotsam are you? You're a pseudo woman, a disgrace to womanhood, living a lads life! Living a lie. You're pathetic. What worth to the world could you be?'

'I have self-worth...' Ruth replied defiantly. 'I must have self-worth. I don't need a man to define me. I define me by doing what I want to do that makes me feel fulfilled. I'm defined by my knowledge, by my upbringing, the things that make me laugh, the things I find fun, fulfilling. I am the substance of what I've read, the films I've watched and my hobbies, my interests and my job. My experiences. I'm a complex person. I am the sum of all those things and more, so of course I have worth.'

*

John looked at his watch, then at the painting of a group of people in a diner, late at night, no one talking to each other. No one, it seemed, was actually with anyone and though it had vivid colours and an almost cartoon feel to it, he couldn't help wonder why she liked it. If he had a wall large enough to put a painting on, he would have had a landscape like The Hay Wain or at least Joseph MW Turner's Margate from the Sea.

The lounge door flew open and he turned from the painting. Ruth rushed in looking down at the floor as she padded across the room in her big socks, craning her neck to look under the sofa.

'I won't be a moment.'

'Sure. Don't worry,' he replied.

'Usually I'm on time.'

'Don't worry about it,' he replied again as he watched her on hands and knees behind the sofa, peering under it.

'It's just that, now that I'm on my own...' She dragged her boots out from under the sofa and sitting on one of the dining chairs, she pulled the first one on.

'I know,' he sympathised. 'I had pretty much the same problem when Michelle left.'

She put the second boot on the table and wiped away a tear as if he had just struck a raw nerve.

'I'm sorry.'

He crossed over to her. 'It's okay. Don't worry. You'll find someone new soon. I'm sure of that.' He put an arm around her shoulder to comfort her.

*

Ruth turned and grabbed another lever. She looked out the window and down the line. The train was still a little way away. She could make out the front of the engine now, but it was still too far away to see any detail.

She glanced back to the schoolgirl.

'If you have self-worth, then pull that lever. If you can really trust yourself to have a meaningful existence on this planet, then do it. See if you are worthy and stop that train.'

*

John was standing by an old fence that stretched across the wood from the river. He heard a splash and turned.

She looked up at him. She was sitting, up to her waist in the fast-flowing water. A cloud of mud billowed and drifted away.

'You alright?'

'Yeah, I'm fine.' She winced. 'Bruised my bum, but otherwise nothing damaged.'

He held onto the tree as he leant towards her, holding out his hand as she stood, and he helped her back onto dry land. He was desperately trying not to laugh as the torrent of water cascaded from her jumper and down her legs.

She wiped the hair from her eyes. As they stood there for a moment looking at each other, a bird was singing overhead somewhere in the canopy.

'You alright?'

'Oh, yes, yes, I've er... found it?'

'Eh?'

'The source of the contamination. There's a pipe probably running back to the works there. Looks like it originally had a cover over it, but that's gone. Probably damaged in a storm or something and now if it rains, the pipe fills when the river swells.'

'And you reckon that every time that happens the flood washes the contaminants into the river?'

'Uh-huh.'

'Great. We'll take a sample from the pipe right away.' She smiled.

'Come on. We'd better get you dry.'

She shook the water out of her sleeves as they began to walk back down the track back to their truck.

'Must be a record, two wet scientists in one day!' She scrunched up the hem of her jumper and squeezed some of the water out as her boots squelched with her every step.

'Must be!' He nodded, they smiled at one another. 'So how's things?'

'Well,' she sighed, 'Simon's doing well at work. He reckons if he maintains his current figures, then he could be in line for a promotion.'

'That's good, isn't it?'

'I suppose. But I don't know.'

They walked on for a dozen or so paces before he asked her, sensing she was holding something from him.

'What?'

'Well, you know how it is?'

'Go on.'

'Well,' she hesitated, wondering how much to tell. 'He's always so busy. I mean, sometimes I wish he'd give the work up and go on the dole or something, because the more he works the less I see of him.' It was like a dam had been breached and she just continued, letting all her concerns flow. 'I mean I love him dearly, but I don't want to have to follow him around like some camp follower all

142

the time, snatching conversations over the phone. That's not a life. I'd be better off on my own. What I wanted it to be like is carefree and fun. I mean, what's the point of being together if you're not having fun? Too many people are too serious. They get in a relationship, based on having a laugh and what do they do? They forget how to have fun. I don't want to repeat the mistakes of my family. I want to live a life, not just live in a life!'

*

She was running down a long, brick tunnel, through the darkness. She could tell there was a rail either side of her and her feet slipped on the wooden sleepers before landing on gravel again.

There was daylight ahead but behind her she could hear a sound of distant thunder, but the rolling sound didn't stop. It got louder and louder and as she turned round, a brilliant white light began to enter the darkness of the tunnel, engulfing quickly the blackened red bricks. The white light rapidly enshrouded her as the roar of thunder became so loud, she couldn't even hear her own mind.

38

She was still holding the lever as the schoolgirl moved the black queen to check the white king.

Ruth smiled.

'My relationship with Simon was over the moment I began to have feelings for someone else. It wasn't his job that pulled us apart, it was my love for someone else. If I had stayed with Simon, then I would have been lying to myself and lying to my soul. No, what happened between him and me was for the best and I am worthy of life because I hold life and happiness above all other wealth. I have found love and I don't intend to lose it.'

*

Ruth's monitor faded down to a single beat.
Then nothing.

*

She pulled the brake lever back and the signal lever unlocked. The schoolgirl turned to the chessboard and then looked up at the clock.

The time was 11:59.

*

The hospital waiting room door opened. They all turned as one and as John rose to his feet, Joe turned to Paul, desperately, his fear almost overwhelming him as the doctor entered.

*

The schoolgirl, transfixed with fear, her eyes staring at Ruth. Her hand swept forward as she was about to say something.

*

The strip light flickered.

'Gentlemen,' the doctor began, 'I've some news about Miss Holland's condition....'

*

The schoolgirl's hand flinched.

Ruth pulled the lever back and there was a loud clanking sound as the signal lever crashed and locked into place.

The white king fell.

The sounds of a steam whistle screamed.

*

Ruth's monitor stopped, and all was silent.

*

John turned anxiously to Paul.
'Gentlemen,' the doctor continued. 'She's going to be just fine.'

*

Her monitor began to beep away as normal. The fingers on her left hand twitched slightly.

*

'We all have worth. We all have love inside us.'

THE END

ABOUT THE AUTHOR

Anthony Day was born in Margate, Kent and now lives in Whitstable writing contemporary, science fiction, fantasy and historically based fiction.

OTHER BOOKS BY THIS AUTHOR INCLUDE

MUNCH

Novella about a monster terrorizing Canterbury suitable for years 9+

THE ADVENTURES OF SAMANTHA BISHOP

Book series set in the 1920's. Following the adventures of two flappers who solve crimes and fight injustice. Suitable for young adults+

CALICO JACK OF THE BLACK FLAG

A series of bawdy comedy shorts about Jack Rackham, Anne Bonny, Mary Read and their crew, plundering the Caribbean Sea.